Shadow Castle

Shadow Castle

by

MARIAN COCKRELL

Illustrated by

OLIVE BAILEY

Whittlesey House

McGRAW-HILL BOOK COMPANY, INC.

New York   *London*

PUBLISHED BY WHITTLESEY HOUSE
A division of the McGraw-Hill Book Company, Inc.

Printed in the United States of America

For LUCINDA *and* KABY, LEACY *and* POOH,
and little LUCY

CONTENTS

CHAPTER 1

The Hidden Tunnel

IF SHE HADN'T GONE EXPLORING in the deep, dark forest, Lucy might never have met the little dog at all. She had always played in the bright woods near her home, and when she wandered very far, and the woods turned into thick forest with deep, black shadows, she always turned back before she got too far into it—that is, she always had before.

Lucy was nine years old and lived with her grandmother in a little white house on the mountainside above the village. She liked living high up where she could look down at the houses, which seemed so little, down at the bottom of the mountain. Some days she went to play with her friends who lived down there, and other days she went up the mountain and wandered about in the woods.

This summer morning she dressed quickly and ran downstairs. "I think I'll go exploring, Grandma," she said while she was eating breakfast. "Could I take some lunch?"

"Why not?" said Grandma. She fixed Lucy some sandwiches and wrapped them in waxed paper. "Be sure and come back before dark," she said.

"I will," Lucy said. "Good-by, Grandma." She took her lunch basket and started off. Lucy liked the woods, the smells and sounds, the little animals that scuttered about in the leaves. She had practiced sitting very still, so that now and then a rabbit or squirrel would come up to her and not be afraid. Usually when she ate lunch she found she had several guests.

But it wasn't time for lunch yet. Lucy slipped along, silently, searching for adventure. Of course if there was any adventure she would have to make it up. She couldn't really have much of an adventure on a mountain where there were no wild animals to be bitten by, no deep streams to drown in, and no steep precipices to fall over.

So she went right on until she came to the dark forest, because how could anybody be an explorer in a place she knew all about already? She had been a little way into the dark forest once before. Today she would go a little farther.

Soon the trees grew more thickly as she went along, the woods became darker as the branches met overhead, shutting out the sunlight, and Lucy began to wonder whether, after all, she really liked exploring.

She found she was walking a little more slowly, in fact she had almost stopped, when a little white dog ran out of the trees in front of her, and stopped and looked at her, wagging his tail.

The little dog had appeared so suddenly that Lucy jumped back before she saw what it was. Then she stood very still, hoping it would stay, because she had wanted a dog for a long time. This one was a round little dog, with a black ear, and a black nose, and bright black eyes. Lucy had never seen him before and was surprised to see a dog this far up the mountain.

"Here, pup! Here, pup!" she called. He didn't have a collar on. Maybe he didn't belong to anybody. Maybe she could take him home. . . .

The little dog came a few steps toward her, gave a friendly little yip, and then turned and trotted off, right into the dark forest. Lucy followed him eagerly.

He turned and looked back every few steps. He didn't seem afraid of her, but he wouldn't come to her. Deeper and deeper into the forest he went, with Lucy after him.

After a while she noticed that they were following a faint path. She didn't remember any path leading into the forest, but here one was. As she went on the trees grew closer and closer together. The forest became darker. Only once in a while did sunlight fall upon the ground.

"I hope I don't get lost," she thought.

She could hear the wind pushing through the tops of the trees. Except for that everything was silent and still. "It's very dim and swishy," she thought. "Maybe I ought to go back."

She looked behind her, and there was the faint trail winding through the trees the way she had come. She looked ahead, and the little dog was almost out of sight.

3

Lucy hurried to catch up with him. "There's no sense in being afraid just because it's dark," she told herself.

All of a sudden the little dog disappeared. Lucy looked everywhere for him, but he was nowhere in sight. Nothing moved but the wind in the trees.

"Here, pup!" she called. "Oh, please come back!"

She heard a sound, a little whine. It was the little dog, saying, "Come on, come on!" But she couldn't see him anywhere.

Then a clump of vines and bushes moved, and a little white head stuck out. Lucy laughed.

"What are you doing in there?" she said.

The little dog whined again, and as Lucy walked toward him his head disappeared again. Lucy parted the vines and looked in.

"Oh!" she said. "Oh, I never knew about *this!*"

She went in after the little dog, and the vines and branches fell back into place, and from the outside no one would have dreamed that . . .

There was a tunnel into the mountain!

Lucy stood still. It was very dark. It didn't exactly look like a good place to go into. "But I wonder where it *goes,*" she said to herself.

Only a little light came through the screen of leaves and vines that hid the entrance to the tunnel. It was just barely high enough for Lucy to stand up in. The little dog whined again.

"But where are we *going?*" Lucy protested. The little dog stood up and put his feet on her dress, then ran into the tunnel, then came back impatiently.

"Well, if you *insist*," Lucy said. She untied her sash and took it off. "Here, come here."

He came this time. He seemed to know that she was going to do what he wanted her to. Lucy tied one end of the sash around his neck. "Go on, then," she said. "But don't go too fast."

The little dog trotted happily into the tunnel, with Lucy behind him. In a moment everything was dark as pitch. Lucy looked back and could just see the faintest glimmer of light where she had come into the tunnel.

The dog led her along with little tugs and jerks. The floor of the tunnel was covered with what felt like soft dust, and their footsteps didn't make any noise at all. There was a damp, chilly, musty feeling in the air, and Lucy felt her heart begin to beat a little faster.

She stopped suddenly and started to turn back. The little dog wouldn't budge. She pulled at the sash. The little dog pulled the other way.

Lucy shivered and went on again. "This is an adventure," she thought. "You can't have an adventure if you stop in the middle." Besides, she didn't want to lose the little dog.

She thought they would never come to the end of this black, cold, creepy tunnel, when all at once she saw in the distance a faint glow of light.

"There's the end!" she thought. The little dog was going faster and faster, so that she was almost running to keep up with him.

Just then they came to a place where the tunnel divided into two passages. The little dog took the left one, and Lucy stopped to look curiously into the one leading off to the right.

The little dog tugged at the sash, and whined. "Hurry, hurry!" he seemed to be saying.

"Wait a minute," Lucy said. Now that she was almost at the end she wasn't in such a hurry to get out. "Let me look." She took a step into the right-hand passage. She was almost sure—she—saw—something—

She did see something. It was coming toward her!

"Ooooooh!" She jumped back quickly as the little dog pulled hard on the other end of the sash. Then with a sudden, fierce growl he leaped at the entrance to the right-hand tunnel, landing just in front of Lucy and barking threateningly. Whatever was there ran back with a faint squeal.

Then the little dog was pulling frantically at the sash again, and they were running, running, for the daylight at the mouth of the tunnel. Lucy sped along wildly, her heart pounding. She was sure she had felt something pull at her arm, trying to drag her into the other passage.

They burst out into the daylight, and Lucy stumbled over a stone and sat down on the ground, breathing heavily and looking over her shoulder again and again. There was nothing to be seen in the black tunnel. The little dog faced back the way they had come, growling softly in his throat.

"What—was—it?" Lucy panted. "What was in there?" The little dog wagged his tail and touched her cheek with his cold nose. "I guess it won't come out," Lucy concluded

in relieved tones, after watching for a few minutes longer.
She began to look around.

There wasn't much to see from her position on the
ground. Everywhere about her was tall, tall grass. Even
when she stood up it was just over her head, and all she
could see were waving green stalks and the sky overhead.
They were in a narrow path that led from the tunnel they
had just left and twisted on ahead of them.

Lucy followed the little dog down this path. "Where on
earth am I?" she thought uneasily. "And how am I ever
going to get home again through that tunnel?" She
glanced back over her shoulder, but the path had turned
and she couldn't even see the hole in the mountain where
the tunnel was. She could see nothing but tall grass.

There was something strange about the place. The air
seemed unreal, as though they were walking through
water. There was a soft greenish-blue haze over everything.

She looked up at the sky. It looked solider than usual.
The sky seemed to be piled on itself, like clear greenish-
blue clouds with the light shining through, beautifully.
It was queer, like a dream. The tall grass rustled and
whispered softly as she passed through it along the narrow path.

Then all at once, around a turn, they came into the
open. Lucy stopped and looked around her. She was in a
valley, which was shaped like a huge bowl, with very steep
sides. High mountains, covered with forest, rose on all
sides, encircling the valley. She saw that the tall waving

7

grass through which she had just come extended all around the edge of the valley, at the foot of the mountains.

The level valley itself was all short, smooth, green grass, with scattered trees and a few large rocks. As she gazed out over this smooth, green lawn, about halfway across the valley on the left side, she saw—a castle!

It was a very large, old, dark, dim castle, made of stone. The forest rose behind it, but its highest towers and turrets stood out against the strange bright sky that seemed to shift and move slowly.

Lucy stared through the clear, unearthly light in a kind of dreamy wonder. A castle, right on, or maybe in, her own mountain where she had lived all her life, and never dreamed of its existence!

Suddenly she realized that the little dog was tugging at the sash she still held in her hand, trying to pull her off to the right. She took her eyes off the castle and turned to see where the little dog was trying to take her now.

She had been so absorbed in looking at the castle that she hadn't even noticed that there was someone else in the valley. Off to the right, not far from the tall grass, was a large flat rock.

On this rock sat a young man.

He had on brown trousers and a bright-green leather jacket exactly the color of the grass, and his hair was red and curly.

The little dog barked and he looked around.

"Hello!" he exclaimed. "How on earth did you find your way in here?" He jumped up from his seat on the rock and grinned at Lucy, as though he were very happy about something.

Lucy came a few steps nearer. "I followed him," she said. She leaned down and unfastened the sash from the little dog's neck and tied it around her waist again. The little dog jumped into the young man's arms and tried to lick his face.

The young man shook his finger at the little dog and said, "And what were you doing outside?"

"He was in the wood," Lucy said. "He wanted me to come, so I did. But there was something in there!" She turned back toward the tunnel. "He barked at it, and—we ran past."

The young man gave a low whistle and frowned angrily in the direction of the tunnel. Then he smiled at Lucy and said, "What's your name?"

"Lucy."

"You can call me Michael, and his name," pointing to the little dog, "is Flumpdoria."

"Flumpdoria," Lucy said. "What a peculiar name. Is he yours?"

"Yes. Do you like him?"

"I think he's wonderful," Lucy said. "I've never had a dog."

"Never had an animal to play with?"

"Oh, yes, I've had lots of animals to play with, but not to keep. I play with the rabbits and squirrels in the woods."

"So you're a friend of the little animals?"

9

I
said
come
looke
ran, f
The
in the
said, "I
th

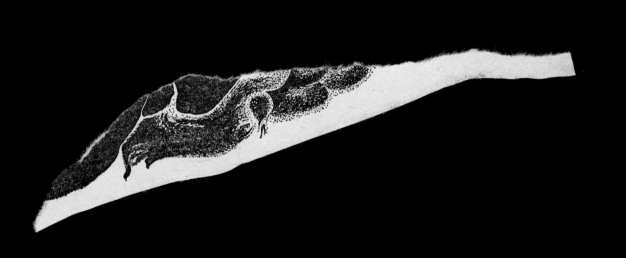

"Yes," said Lucy. "I'm in the woods all the time, but I never knew about this."

"I see," said Michael.

"It feels—queer—in here." Lucy stared at the tall grass. "It whispers," she said.

"Yes," said Michael.

"Do you live there?" Lucy nodded toward the castle.

"I have, for a long time," Michael said. The happy, excited look came on his face again.

"It looks so dark. Is it—haunted?"

"In a way it is," he answered. "Would you like to go in?"

"Er—not very much," Lucy admitted. "I'd go with you, though."

"There's nothing there to hurt you," Michael said. "Just dust and shadows. I'll take you through. It will make the time pass more quickly while I'm waiting."

"What are you waiting for?" Lucy asked, but Michael didn't answer.

They walked across the grass toward the castle. Lucy didn't want to go very much, hardly at all in fact, but at the same time she felt she simply had to know what was inside. Flumpdoria waggled along behind them.

When they were close to it, the castle towered above them and looked larger than ever. They entered a great, high-ceilinged hall, so high that Lucy could hardly see the ceiling at all. Some light streamed in through small, narrow windows high in the wall. Cobwebs hung from great beams and shone where the shafts of light from the windows hit them. Lucy edged closer to Michael.

11

"It would take too long to show you the whole thing," Michael said. "The only really interesting part of it is up here."

He opened a small door on the right, and they passed into a bedroom that looked very old but was clean and neat, as though the owner had just stepped out. Lucy thought that this must be where Michael lived.

They didn't stop, though, but went across the room to a little door. It was painted greenish-blue, and queerly shaped iron hinges held it to the wall. Michael shot back a bolt and tugged at the door. It didn't budge.

"I haven't been up here in years," he said, straining to force the door open. "Stubborn thing!" He stood for a moment quietly, then suddenly yanked at the handle and the door flew open, almost throwing him to the floor. "There!" he said triumphantly. "He was holding it closed for spite."

Lucy wondered if there had been someone on the other side of the door, holding it closed. There was no one there now. Then she noticed the handle.

"What a queer door handle," she said. "It looks like a goblin's head."

"It is," said Michael. "That's a Nit-goblin. They're very unintelligent. He doesn't like to be disturbed."

"Oh, was *he* holding the door? Is he alive?"

"Yes, more or less. Stupid idiot!"

Lucy was almost sure she saw the goblin make a horrible face at Michael as they passed through the doorway. They were at the foot of a steep, circular stairway.

At first it was so dim that she couldn't see anything at

all, but after her eyes became accustomed to the faint
light she saw that the stairs were dusty and covered with
cobwebs and barely wide enough for them to go up in
single file. It was impossible to dodge all the cobwebs that
swung slowly from the walls, and she kept having to brush
them off her face. The stair wound up and up.

They climbed and climbed, and the steps seemed end-
less.

"We're in the tallest tower," Michael said. "I'm glad
you came. I haven't had any company for some time."

"Is there any way out except through the dark tunnel?"
Lucy asked.

"Don't you worry about the tunnel," Michael said. "I
won't let them hurt you."

"Who?" she asked, but they had at last arrived at the
top and Michael didn't answer. They were standing before another little greenish-blue door, just like the other
one, with a goblin's-head handle. This goblin had its eyes
closed, however, and the door swung half open.

"*Anyone* could get in here!" Michael said angrily.
"Lazy thing."

"He seems to have a better disposition than the other
one," Lucy remarked.

"He'd be just as disagreeable if he could stay awake
long enough to take the trouble," Michael said, slamming
the door hard. "Let's sit over here."

He led Lucy to a long, low seat, covered with soft,
dusty velvet, with tarnished gold tassels at either end.
They sat down and Flumpdoria flopped at their feet.

"Tell me what you see," Michael said.

13

Lucy looked about the room. She didn't see anything much at first but old dusty furniture and old heavy draperies here and there. There were two large windows, but vines grew all over them, so that they didn't let in much light. There was nothing else but dust and shadows. Lucy was disappointed.

Then she began to wonder.

What made the shadows?

They moved across the room and disappeared, and others took their places. And every one of them was the shadow of a person. They walked about soundlessly and appeared to gesture and talk to one another.

"Michael!" Lucy whispered softly, touching his arm. He was smiling vaguely, as though he thought of something far away. "Michael, who makes the shadows?"

Michael looked down at her and smiled. "They're the shadows of people who have lived in this castle," he said. "It's part of the magic."

"Then—it *is* enchanted! I *felt* there was something odd about it!"

Michael was silent again, and Lucy followed the direction of his eyes. He was watching the shadow of a young girl as it moved about. She seemed very beautiful and graceful. She wore long robes, with sleeves that fell to the floor, and her hair was long, hanging to her knees.

She was walking back and forth, and every once in a while Lucy thought she held out her arms in their direction.

"What does she want?" she whispered. "Is she trying to tell us something?"

"She's tired of waiting," Michael said, "for the enchantment to be over. She gets very impatient sometimes. That is Gloria, the first princess who ever lived here. This castle was made for her."

"Was she a—Fairy Princess?"

"Well, not at first. Would you like to hear about her?"

"Oh, *yes!*" said Lucy.

CHAPTER 2

The Magical Rescue

"IT BEGAN THIS WAY," MICHAEL said, gazing into the shadows as he talked. Some of the shadows flickered about. Others moved more slowly and almost seemed to come into the middle of the room. But you couldn't tell. You couldn't quite tell.

Curiosity started it (he went on), as it does most things, and the curiosity belonged to Prince Mika. Mika was a Fairy Prince, but he didn't like it very much. A prince can do or have whatever he wants, so people think, but it isn't true at all when you have forty-seven older brothers.

Being the youngest of forty-eight can be very trying, even if they're all princes. If Mika wanted to give a ball in the main ballroom, he couldn't do it unless none of the other princes wanted to give one that night, so you can

see that he was practically never able to have a party
when he wanted to.

If he had just finished a beautiful experiment and had
managed to change a toad into three white mice with rib-
bons on their tails, as likely as not one of his brothers
would come along and change them into six bats with
long, green feathers before he could enjoy his experiment.

So he was nearly always in a state of frustration, and
it's no wonder he decided to travel. His father, King
Klux, ruler of the Fairies of Forest and Wild, thought
it was a good idea, and said he wouldn't mind if all his
sons decided to travel.

Mika hurried off before any of his brothers should decide to go with him, and he stopped to see his godmother,
Flumpdoria.

"Flumpdoria! He was named after the Prince's godmother, wasn't he?" Lucy said excitedly.

Flumpdoria heard his name and wriggled a little, and
climbed into her lap.

"Yes," Michael said. "It pleased her. She's very fond
of animals."

"Go on about the Prince," said Lucy.

Well, the Prince went to see his godmother. She was
very busy directing a great many fairies in the making
of a bridal gown for the future wife of Prince Mara,
Mika's sixteenth-from-the-oldest brother.

"Hello," said Flumpdoria. "What do you want so early in the morning?"

"I'm going away," Mika said. "I'm going to travel."

"You ought to be married," Flumpdoria said. "Then you wouldn't be so restless."

"Married!" said Mika. "I can't marry until all my brothers have chosen their wives, and there's no one left but a few of those hook-nosed pale-green swamp witches, and even though they are princesses everybody knows they're half goblin."

Flumpdoria sighed. "You're so difficult, Mika. It's unfortunate that you happened to be born last, of course, but. . . . Oh, well, where do you want to go on your travels?"

"I want to see all the world."

"There's a good deal of it," Flumpdoria said. "You might visit the Kingdom of the Cloud Fairies, and the Fire Fairies, and the River Fairies, but for heaven's sake don't go falling in love with a mermaid. They're never happy anywhere except in the water."

"I don't want to see them," Mika said scornfully. "I want to see mortals. I want to go all over everywhere and see things I've never seen before."

"I was afraid of that," Flumpdoria said with a sigh. "Well, take this magical mouse with you, and if you ask him he will make you any shape you want to be, or entirely invisible. I know you'll be in trouble of some kind before very long. Do try to behave yourself, and don't try any of your magical experiments on a mortal. They don't like it."

"You must be back in six months. Good luck."

"Thanks a lot, Flumpy," Mika said, kissing her. "I knew you'd help me out."

He hurried away, with the magical mouse, in a tiny golden cage, hanging from his waist by a chain. It was a very small mouse, only about half an inch long. Of course Prince Mika was very small too, only about eight inches high, though that is rather large for a fairy. Some of the Flower Fairies, for instance, are no larger than the mouse.

Mika went through this very valley, which is enchanted and is the fairies' entrance to the outer world. He went through the tunnel, which opens into the goblin kingdoms, and there were some goblins working in the passage.

"Mouse, make me a bat," he said, and immediately he was turned into a bat and flew past. He was in such a hurry to see the world that he didn't want to stop and fight goblins, who have always been enemies of the fairies.

When he came out into the dark forest the mouse gave him his own form again. He wandered around for a while, and finally came upon some men with dark-red skins and very few clothes, dancing around a fire. He was very much surprised at their being so large, but a fairy can be any size he wants to, so Mika grew until he was as tall as they were.

He stood watching them until they saw him, and then they all ran away very fast.

"Silly things," he thought. "I'll go to another country."

This was a very long time ago, and there were no people

in this country but primitive Indians, but Mika didn't know that at the time.

The West Wind was blowing past just then, and Mika jumped into his windy arms and let himself be carried along.

"I want to see the world," he said. "Where are you going?"

"Straight east," said the West Wind. "Come along if you want to. If you see a place you'd like to stop I'll let you down."

"Thank you," said Mika. It was quite comfortable rushing through the air with the West Wind, and they went on together for days.

The West Wind told him that all mortals were not like the primitive Indians, so Mika stayed with him and rode over a vast ocean. After they had crossed the ocean they went on to a far country and came to a great city, with gleaming towers and a wall around it.

"This looks interesting," Mika said. "I think I'd like to stop here. Thank you very much for bringing me."

"I enjoyed having you," said the West Wind. "I'll be around for a few days if you should need me." He set Mika down on the streets of the city, waved good-by, and went on his way.

Mika looked about him. "Why, no one has any wings," he said to himself. "Mouse, take my wings away, please." He didn't want to look different from everyone else.

There were great crowds on each side of the street, and Mika saw that the reason for this was that a procession was coming.

"What is it?" Mika asked a man standing near him.

"It's King Torros," the man said, "returning from the wars with his captives. You must be a traveler from far away, or you'd know that."

"I am," Mika said. They could understand each other perfectly, because fairies speak all the languages in the world without even knowing it.

Mika didn't pay much attention to King Torros, though, for when the procession came up to where he was, he saw, riding behind the King on a white horse, the most beautiful girl he had ever dreamed of. There were golden chains on her wrists and ankles.

"Is she a captive?" he asked the man he had spoken to before.

"Yes," said the man. "She is the daughter of His Majesty's enemy, King Ferdinand. She is to marry King Torros's son."

"What does the son look like?" Mika asked.

"He is the Crown Prince," the man answered discreetly.

"Make me invisible," Mika said to the mouse, and the mouse did so at once. Mika saw the man he had been talking to looking about for him with a startled expression on his face.

Mika walked along beside the beautiful Princess. She looked very sad, and it made him sad to watch her.

When the procession reached the palace, he heard the King tell his soldiers to put her in the highest tower room. Mika asked the mouse for his wings again and flew up to

the highest window in the highest tower and perched on the sill.

Very soon the door of the room opened and the Princess was thrust inside. Mika was still invisible, so she didn't see him.

She had been there only a few minutes when the Crown Prince came up to speak to his new bride. Of all the brutish, idiotic creatures Mika had ever seen, he was the worst. He was fat, with black hair growing nearly down to his eyebrows, little piggish eyes, a turned-up snout, and dark, discolored teeth.

The Princess drew back from him in tactless horror. This didn't bother the Crown Prince at all. He was evidently used to it. He made some remarks about the wedding being tomorrow, but withdrew hastily when the Princess threw a footstool at him.

Mika chuckled admiringly. He liked the way she handled the situation. "Make me visible, mouse," he whispered.

He slid from the window sill into the room and appeared before the Princess.

"Gracious!" she said. "How on earth did you get here?"

"I came through the window," Mika explained.

The Princess looked out. The tower room was several hundred feet from the ground. "Hmmmmm," she said.

"I am Prince Mika. I'll take you away if you want me to."

"There's nothing I'd like better," she said. "My name is Gloria."

23

"I fell in love with you the minute I saw you riding along the street," Mika said, not wasting any time.

Gloria smiled at him. "I've always liked red hair."

"I got my red hair from my mother," Mika said. "She was a Fire Princess."

"Oh," said Gloria. "Then you're not . . . ?"

"No, I'm not a mortal." Mika was a little worried. "But you come with me. I'd like awfully to marry you. I'm sure Flumpdoria will help me arrange it some way."

"Who's Flumpdoria?"

"She's my godmother."

"It sounds wonderful, but how are you going to get me out?" Gloria asked.

"I think," Mika said, "that if you'd hold my hand and not let go we could just go out the window."

"You *think* so!" Gloria exclaimed indignantly. "If I'm going to learn to fly, I'd rather start from the ground. Then if it doesn't work, I'll still be all in one piece."

"It was just a suggestion," Mika said. "Anyway, I'll come and get you before they have you married to him. Don't worry, now."

He slid out the window to go and think of a plan for rescuing Gloria. She stood looking at the spot where he had been, and hoped she hadn't been dreaming.

Mika went out over the country and made a test to be sure the flying business would work. He picked up a baby pig and carried it through the air. He let it go over a convenient haystack, and found that as soon as he wasn't touching it, it fell to the ground. The pig slid squealing down the haystack and ran away. Mika started looking for his friend the West Wind.

All that night Gloria wondered about the young man who had appeared in her tower room so mysteriously. She couldn't decide whether she had been dreaming or not, but she got up very early so as to be ready in case he came. Ever since she had been made prisoner by King Torros she had been trying to think of some way to escape.

One look at the Crown Prince had been almost too much for her. She kept looking out of the tower window, and thinking that she would jump out if worse came to worst, though it was a terribly long way to the ground. But there was no use doing that unless it was absolutely necessary, so she kept waiting a few more minutes for Mika to appear and save her.

Then the ladies-in-waiting came to dress her for the wedding, and she didn't have a chance to jump out of the window if she wanted to. She just couldn't keep still while they were arranging her hair, so finally they turned her around so she could face the window. Then she stood very still and looked and looked for Mika, but he didn't come.

When she was all dressed it was time for the wedding.

"I won't go," said Gloria.

"Oh, you must," all the ladies said together, and they dragged her out of the room.

"You'll love the Prince when you get used to him," they said.

"You're the most beautiful princess we've had in the palace in years."

"The Prince is out hunting for weeks at a time."

Gloria didn't think any one of them sounded as though she'd like to marry the Prince herself, though, and decided he must be even worse than he looked, if possible, because there is hardly ever a Crown Prince, no matter how ugly, who can't find a great many ladies who would like to marry him.

"His ears look like toadstools," she protested as they dragged her down the stairs.

"Oh, nooooooo!" said the ladies.

"I know he's an idiot," she wailed.

"He's very, *very* clever," said the ladies.

"Well, I just won't marry him," she said firmly.

"But you simply must," they said, as they dragged her into the large hall where the wedding guests were assembled. It was a very undignified way for a bride to appear at her wedding, but it was the only way the ladies could think of to get Gloria to appear at all.

As Gloria was being dragged to where the Prince waited for her, smiling horribly, a strong wind swept through the hall. It was the West Wind, whom Mika had persuaded to help him again. Mika was riding with him, but he was invisible.

He swept in through the great open doors, circled the hall, and swept out again, bearing Gloria in his arms. It was really very easy. As neither Mika nor the West Wind was visible, the wedding guests were quite mystified as to what caused the bride to sail through the air and out of the palace in so unusual a manner.

Everyone ran out, and there was much waving of arms

and shouting, but Gloria had sailed out of sight before anyone could decide what to do about it.

"This is fun!" Gloria exclaimed delightedly as they flew along through the air. "I never thought I'd be able to fly. I thought you were never coming."

"I was busy," Mika said. "I was talking to your father."

"Father! Where is he?"

"We're going to see him now. I had a long talk with him. King Torros had him shut up in a dungeon. I knew a magic spell for unlocking doors, and freed him and all the other captives. King Torros is going to be surprised when he finds his dungeons empty of everything but rats and lizards."

"That's simply wonderful," Gloria said. "What did you talk to Father about?"

"You. He said if you wanted to marry me he'd give his consent, but goodness only knew what would come of it."

"Sounds just like him," Gloria remarked.

Just then the West Wind set them down in a large grove of trees, many miles from the King's palace. Many people were wandering about, captives whom Mika had released from the dungeons and brought here. Mika thanked the West Wind, and he went puffing away.

He led Gloria across the grove to where her father was standing, and she rushed to him with cries of joy. He kissed her, and they were so glad to see each other that they almost forgot about Mika for a few moments. Then King Ferdinand turned around and saw Mika and said,

"Oh. Yes. Er—hmmmm." And Gloria just looked at Mika and didn't say anything.

Then the King said, "Gloria, do you want to marry this man?"

Gloria said, "Well—er—yes. On the whole I think I do."

"It's extremely sudden," said her father.

"Well, I do, anyway," Gloria murmured.

"I'm sure I don't know what the Queen will say, if we ever find her," sighed King Ferdinand.

"The West Wind told me that the South Wind said that King Torros left her at home," Mika said, "because she talked so much."

"We can settle this much better without her," the King said. "If you are determined, we'll go back to my kingdom right away and have the wedding."

"We couldn't possibly do that," Mika said hastily. "We can't be married at all until I go and see my godmother. A marriage with a mortal has to be arranged."

"What next?" the King sighed. "Still, it's not a bad idea to have a magician in the family. I've always wanted to study magic."

"After we're married, we'll come and visit you, and I'll teach you all the magic I can," Mika promised. "I'll have to learn a good deal more myself if I stay around mortals very long," he added. "They get into so many difficulties."

"How shall we get back home?" asked King Ferdinand.

"Over there behind that clump of trees," Mika said, "are all King Torros's best horses and coaches and everything you need for a pleasant journey. He can't pursue you because he has nothing to ride on. We must be going. Come on, Gloria."

Gloria ran to kiss her father good-by and to assure him that she'd be back as soon as possible.

Then Mika led her away, a little worried as to what Flumpdoria was going to say to this.

CHAPTER 3

The Enchantment

IKA AND GLORIA RODE
home on a cloud, because Mika thought Gloria would
be more comfortable traveling this way than riding the
wind. They had one minor accident. Mika forgot that
Gloria needed help in order to sail through the air so easily and let go her hand for a moment to point at something beneath them. He just barely managed to catch her
as she began to fall.

Gloria was so upset by this that she insisted on tying
their wrists together, in case Mika should become absent-
minded again. It made moving about rather difficult, but
Gloria said she liked it that way, and didn't mind the in-
convenience. There wasn't much use in moving about on
the cloud, anyway, as it was all just alike.

After not many days they came to the valley, and the
cloud settled to the ground near a large rock.

"You sit on this rock and wait for me, darling," Mika said, "while I go and see about our wedding. I'm sure it won't be very hard to manage."

"Wait here?" Gloria exclaimed. "All alone?"

"I *can't* take you with me, sweetheart," Mika said. "Wear this bracelet, and I'll draw a ring around you, and nothing can get in to hurt you." Mika drew a circle around the rock, and said, "El bingo swozzlebop bingo el," very fast. Then he kissed her hastily and disappeared before she could answer.

He reappeared again a moment later, though, to kiss her good-by again, and then was gone. Gloria waited a few moments to see if he'd come back again, but this time nothing happened.

She looked all around, but nothing was in sight but trees and grass and the mountains that ringed the valley.

"I hope this turns out all right," she thought. "I'm sure I could never find my way home again." She slipped the bracelet he had given her onto her arm.

Immediately she began to see things she hadn't been able to see before. All about the rock, just outside the ring Mika had drawn in the grass, were horrid little men about a foot high, looking at her curiously and making faces.

Gloria was terribly frightened, and took the bracelet off quickly, but put it on again right away.

"I wish I hadn't put it on," she thought. "But I'll have to wear it now, for since I know they are there, it's more uncomfortable *not* to see them."

"Who are you?" she called to them. "What do you want?"

31

They didn't say a word, just danced around her and shook their fists. But they never came inside the ring, so at last Gloria wasn't frightened any more, and she got tired and went to sleep.

In the meantime Mika was causing a good deal of excitement in Fairyland. He went first to Flumpdoria and told her that he simply had to marry Gloria, and couldn't she please do something about it.

"I knew something would happen," Flumpdoria said. "Your father will be simply wild. But we'll have to try to get his consent. It will be very difficult if we don't."

"She's of royal birth," Mika said hopefully.

"She's a mortal, isn't she?" asked his godmother scornfully. "*That's* what makes it hard. And she may not agree to the conditions. However, let's go and see your father. I'm quite certain he won't be any help at all."

They jumped into Flumpdoria's chariot and rushed to the palace. King Klux was sitting on his throne, listening to the report of the royal gardener.

"Good day, Your Majesty," said Flumpdoria. "Mika wants to be married."

"Well, well," said the King, "I'm glad you've finally decided to be sensible. I have your wife all picked out."

"I've already selected one for myself," Mika said. "A princess."

"I'll have to see her myself," said the King. "Still, if she's a princess. . . ."

"The only trouble is," Flumpdoria put in, "she's a mortal, so of course we'll need your help."

"A mortal!" roared King Klux. "Are you crazy? Go away! Get out! You can't marry a mortal, and that's final! Of all the idiotic, senseless, impertinent. . . ."

"It can be done, you know," Flumpdoria interrupted.

"It *won't* be done!" cried King Klux, jumping up and down in a frenzy. The royal gardener retired with no noise at all, to spread the report among the fairies that Prince Mika wanted to marry a mortal.

"You don't want him marrying one of those swamp princesses, do you?" said Flumpdoria. "Imagine having the damp creature slithering around the palace!"

"I *will not* consent! To think that a son of mine could be so. . . ."

"We'd better go," said Flumpdoria to Mika. "I knew it wouldn't do any good to consult him. Come with me and we'll solve the problem some way. He'll be too busy to interfere much, because he'll soon be in a war with the Swamp King. He had your marriage arranged for, you see, with the eldest Swamp Princess, and your refusal to marry her will surely lead to a battle."

"I told him ages ago I wouldn't marry her," said Mika.

When they arrived at Flumpdoria's house she went to the attic and began dragging old dusty books from the shelves.

"I'll have to look up the magic," she said. "This hasn't been done in a long time, if ever."

She sat down at a table, with books piled high around her, and began looking through them rapidly, searching for some information concerning marriage with mortals.

Dust rose from the books and swirled about her, dancing and glittering wherever the light struck it.

Mika leaned over her shoulder curiously, repeating softly to himself some of the incantations he read there. At once there were faint rustlings and sighs in the air.

"Stop, stop!" Flumpdoria cried. "You silly thing, do you want all the jinns and genii in the world bumping about in this room? Don't say those spells aloud. And stop looking over my shoulder. It gives me the creeps."

"Sorry," said Mika. "I didn't think."

"If you want to help, take this book and go over there and see what you can find in it. If there's nothing here on the subject, we'll have to consult Glauz."

Mika didn't read aloud any more, and for a while the silence was broken only by the turning of the leaves of the big books. Every time a leaf was turned, clouds of dust rose in the still air, for these books were not used once in a thousand years. The magic in them was very strong, for special occasions, and only an accomplished magician knew how to use it.

After a while Flumpdoria stood up with a sigh. "I have it," she said. "I thought it was here. But I'll have to get Glauz to help me. I don't think I can do this by myself."

So she and Mika got into the chariot again, and swiftly rode to Glauz's house. Glauz was the foremost magician of the kingdom, and knew about all kinds of magic.

He lived in a beautiful rose-crystal cave, with many rooms hung with wonderful tapestries. As Flumpdoria and Mika descended from the chariot he came to meet them and took them into his reception room.

"I have something really interesting to consult you about," Flumpdoria said. "Mika wants to marry a mortal."

"A mortal!" The old magician looked at Mika severely over his square spectacles. "Young man, you're going to cause a good deal of trouble if you continue to have notions like that."

"I won't have any more like it," Mika said, "if we can just get this one worked out."

"The King won't like it," said Glauz.

"He's in a dreadful pet already," Flumpdoria said. "We must hurry, before he takes steps to prevent the marriage."

Flumpdoria beckoned to the footmen on the chariot, and they took out the huge book of magic and carried it into the crystal cave.

"Bring it into my workroom," Glauz said. "I think better in there." The workroom was almost entirely filled with books, so that there was hardly room left for a table and chair. They sent Mika outside.

"You're only in the way. We'll call you when we're ready."

Mika wandered around outside, kicking at stones and trying to be patient. He hoped Gloria wasn't getting tired of waiting.

After a long time Flumpdoria came out of the crystal cave looking very tired.

"I had to promise him one of my best and oldest books on deep blue magic," she said, "to get him to help us."

"You're an old darling," Mika said, kissing her on her ear, which always tickled her and made her jump.

"Stop it. No nonsense! We must go to Gloria this minute."

They entered the chariot, and Glauz hurried out and got in too. He had the strangest collection of things with him: three small purple flowers, two very young tadpoles, a red feather and a blue one, a bottle of something labeled "Magic Sprinkle," two unwieldy rainbows that kept knocking them in the head, and so many other things that they could hardly find room for all of them. They packed them all in, though, and set out for the valley where Mika had left Gloria.

Gloria was sleeping soundly, curled up on the rock, when they arrived. She sat up quickly and looked around. There, standing beside her, were an old woman dressed in beautiful robes, Mika, and an old man with his arms full of all sorts of things. His face was mostly white whiskers, except for the piercing green eyes behind his spectacles. The goblins were gone.

"This is my godmother," Mika said, kissing Gloria, "and the great magician Glauz. They're going to help us."

Gloria slipped off the rock and curtsied.

"Do you really want to marry him?" Flumpdoria asked.

"Yes," Gloria said timidly.

"There are conditions you must both agree to. You, Gloria, will never die. You will live your natural life here with Mika, and then you will come to Fairyland.

"Mika, you will be changed to a mortal, more or less. You'll have to stay the same large size. You will have no

36

wings. And *you* cannot return to Fairyland for a thousand years and seven days. After Gloria comes to Fairyland, she will begin her education, and will study all the fairy things she doesn't know, until the thousand years and seven days are over, when you will come back to Fairyland and be reunited forever. Do you agree?"

"It seems an awfully long time," Gloria said, "but I agree."

"The time will pass much more quickly for you in Fairyland than it will for Mika among the mortals," Glauz said. "Mika?"

"I agree," said Mika, wondering what he was going to do with himself for a thousand years and seven days.

Then Glauz and Flumpdoria waved their wands and drew a circle in the grass. A brilliant light shot up from the center of the circle, and Glauz put into it one by one all the things he had brought with him, and every time he put in something else the light changed color.

It was very beautiful, and, when they were told to, Gloria and Mika repeated some words they didn't understand and hand in hand stepped into the center of the circle. All about them was the brilliant changing light, enveloping them, so that for a few moments they could see nothing else.

Then, suddenly, the light was gone and the circle was gone, and they were standing on the grass beside the big rock.

"Look behind you," Flumpdoria said. They turned, and there was a beautiful castle, with flags flying from the tur-

rets, and servants running about making sure that things were ready for them.

"Well, you're married," Flumpdoria said, sighing. "If your father makes too much fuss, I may come and visit you for a while. There's a library there, Mika. You might spend some time studying. I've lent you some of my best books."

"You may have trouble with goblins," Glauz warned them, "living so near the goblin country. Be careful. You're a nice child," he added to Gloria. "When you come to Fairyland, I shall take great pleasure in instructing you myself."

Gloria turned to thank them, but where Flumpdoria and Glauz had been standing, there was only a faint glow, and this disappeared while she looked at it.

Mika put his arm around her waist and they walked slowly toward the castle.

"It's much finer than my father's palace," Gloria said.

They walked across the lawn and into the great hall, where the servants, standing in a line, curtsied to them, smiling. You could hardly tell they were not mortal, Gloria thought, except for the fact that they all had such very bright green eyes. They were all as large as she was.

They explored the castle, which was furnished with lovely things, and got settled in it very quickly. The fairies made Gloria beautiful clothes, because she had come away with nothing except what she had on.

They were very happy and silly, because they loved each other so much, and the time passed quickly. Mika, as

Flumpdoria had suggested, spent some time each day reading magic in the library.

After a while they went on a visit to King Ferdinand, as they had promised. He was overjoyed to see them, as was Queen Katrina, Gloria's mother. She liked Mika, and forgave him for taking her daughter away so suddenly.

They went to parties and balls, and enjoyed their visit very much. After that, they would visit each other every once in a while, but Queen Katrina was never very comfortable in the fairy castle, and her servants never got along very well with the fairy servants. Besides, she didn't like the idea of being transported halfway around the world in a few seconds, although the King always said he thought it a very sensible way to travel.

Sometimes King Ferdinand came by himself, and he and Mika spent long hours in the library. The King got to be fairly proficient in the simpler forms of magic, and became quite famous in his own country as a magician.

Michael stopped talking, and Lucy sat quietly, watching the shadows and thinking of all the things she had heard. The longer she watched them, the more the shadows seemed to move and circle about her in a haze.

"It's not comfortable when it's so quiet," she said at last. "The air gets purple."

"It does, doesn't it?" Michael said. "The first time Gloria came up here she said immediately that there was something strange about this room. They didn't know about the shadows then."

"Did they live happily ever after?" Lucy asked. "Had

they any children? Are they in Fairyland now, this minute?"

"Gloria is. She's still there, waiting for Mika. You see, the thousand years and seven days aren't up yet."

"Ooooh! And that's why she gets tired of waiting. And does Mika ever come and see her shadow? Can she talk? To him?"

"No, she can't talk to him," Michael said. "If she had her shadow with her, it would do everything she does, as shadows always do. And that's what it does in this room. Mika comes sometimes and watches the shadow to see what she's doing, but it makes him homesick. He wants to see Gloria, and of course he can't. When it's a cloudy day in Fairyland, there isn't any shadow in this room."

"Who are the other shadows, Michael?"

"They are shadows of the members of Mika's and Gloria's family, who are now in Fairyland."

"So they did have some children?"

"Yes. They had two. A little girl named Meira, for the Queen, Mika's mother, and a little boy named Robin. Of course when the children were born—they were twins— King Klux forgave Mika for marrying a mortal and came to the great feast to celebrate. Things almost went wrong again, though, when they didn't name the boy Klux.

"But Gloria said she wouldn't consent to his having a name like that under any circumstances. Mika told his father that, really, since all his forty-seven older brothers had named their firstborn after the King, it would avoid confusion to have him called something else.

"King Ferdinand, who was there, too, pointed out that

they hadn't named the child after him either, so King Klux was comforted, and said no more about it. He and King Ferdinand took quite a liking to each other.

"Queen Katrina came, of course, and brought with her a woman who had been Gloria's nurse when she was a baby. Her name was Nancy Belle, and she was to look after the babies. It turned out she wasn't much use, but Gloria liked having her around. Nancy Belle couldn't tell a grasshopper from a fairy, but she was a good old thing."

"Are Robin's and Meira's shadows here?"

"That's Robin over there. See that young man waving a wand? I think he's performing some kind of magic. Robin had an unfortunate experience with goblins, and later became interested in the subject of goblin magic, and specialized in it. He knows more about that kind of magic than anyone in the kingdom."

When Michael stopped talking, the shadows became darker, and Lucy watched the shadow of Robin making strange motions with his wand. It was queer to think that she was seeing the shadow of something that was actually happening right this minute. Something in *Fairyland!*

"Could you tell me about Robin's unfortunate experience?" she asked.

Michael got up and went to the window, pushing aside the vines to look up at the late morning sun.

"I'll tell you about it," he said. "It's early. Time seems to go very slowly today."

Lucy sat very still and quiet, waiting. The strange purple light seemed to grow dense. The shadows looked almost solid, as though they were real people. They passed and repassed each other, and it was hard to keep her eyes on one shadow.

Then Michael began to talk softly, and the light became less purple, and the shadows seemed thinner, until Lucy wasn't seeing them at all, but thinking of the castle as it used to be, with things happening in it.

CHAPTER 4

The Visiting Princess

S THE CHILDREN GREW UP (Michael said) it was easy to see that there was a difference between them. Robin was very like his father, with red curly hair and green eyes, while Meira was like her mother, golden-haired and blue-eyed. You could hardly tell she was half fairy, she looked and acted so much like a mortal.

One summer when they were about twenty years old, Meira went for a visit to her grandparents, King Ferdinand and Queen Katrina, in their kingdom of Kengaria, but Robin stayed at home. He was a great favorite with all the fairies, and liked to be with them.

One day Flumpdoria appeared at the castle for a conference with Mika and Gloria. She stepped out of her carriage, which disappeared, and immediately grew to mortal size, as she usually did when in the castle, as a matter of convenience.

"It's time the boy was married," she said, "and even if it isn't, everyone seems to think it is. I'm always being hinted at by ambassadors from this country or that, about how beautiful or accomplished their particular princess is."

"I won't have him marry except for love," Gloria said decidedly.

"Certainly not. But we could invite a princess here to visit, and he might fall in love with her."

So that's what they decided to do, and after much consideration decided on the only daughter of the King of the Blue Elves. She was reported to be the most beautiful and the most intelligent and to have the sweetest disposition.

They sent gifts and messages, and invited her to come to the castle and make them a visit. In a few days there was an answer accepting the invitation.

Everything in Blue Elfland is blue—trees, grass, flowers, everything. It is the national color. So Gloria prepared a room especially for the Princess, all in blue.

Then they were ready for their visitor, whose name was Bluebell, and after three days a messenger arrived to say that the Princess would be there at any moment.

Soon a beautiful, tiny chariot, drawn by bright blue dragonflies, stopped in front of the castle. The Princess stepped out, waved a wand, and she and the chariot and all her company, in the twinkling of an eye, became as large as mortals.

Mika and Gloria and Robin went out to meet the Princess. She was very beautiful, with cloudy black hair and deep blue eyes, but Mika didn't think she was as beauitful as Gloria.

She greeted them ceremoniously, and they escorted her into the castle, where she exclaimed over her lovely blue room, and seemed altogether pleased to be there.

No one told Robin the reason the Princess Bluebell had been invited to the castle, but he probably had a pretty good idea anyway. He was very polite to her. He danced with her and walked with her, but he didn't seem to be seeking her out when it wasn't necessary for politeness' sake.

The Princess didn't seem to be very fond of the daytime. The only things she really enjoyed were the dances that were held at night. She always wore beautiful blue gowns. She slept late in the mornings, and her little maid carried her breakfast to her.

This maid was an ugly, shy little thing. Her skin was a deep purple, and she never said a word. The Princess said that the little maid couldn't talk, and that she was very sorry for her.

One night, when the Princess had been there about a week, Robin went up to his mother's rooms to see her just before dinner. He was surprised to see Gloria still sitting before her dressing table, with her maid arranging her hair.

"Why, Mother, you're late, aren't you?"

"Hello, darling," Gloria said. "Yes, I am. Everything's gone wrong today."

The maid, who was combing her hair, pulled nervously at the comb, and Gloria said, "Oh, you hurt me."

"I'm sorry, Your Highness. I didn't mean to."

"It's all right. What's the matter with you tonight, Tinkle? You're so jumpy."

"I—I don't know, Your Highness. Something is queer —I—don't know. Oh, I *can't* get your hair right!" And Tinkle began to cry.

"See?" Gloria said to Robin. "Every single soul in the castle has been acting strangely all day. *I* don't know what's the matter with them. There, Tinkle, that's all right. It looks very nice. Go and get your dinner, and maybe you'll feel better!"

Tinkle set a diadem of pearls on her mistress's head. Gloria looked lovely. She looked just the same as she had when she and Mika were married. Because of the fairy spell, she never grew old.

"Tinkle," she said, "if there's anything wrong, I think I ought to know about it, don't you?"

Tinkle looked unhappy, and said, "Yes, Your Highness. But I don't know what it is. Everything's queer."

That was all she would say, so Gloria told her to run along.

"I wonder what's the matter with her," she said when Tinkle had gone. "She's dropped everything she picked up, she brought me the wrong slippers, it took her two hours to do my hair, and I am simply exhausted."

"She's not the only one," Robin said. "All the servants keep looking over their shoulders. That is, all of ours. The ones the Princess brought with her don't seem to be bothered. You don't suppose they've been quarreling with each other, do you?"

"I wish I knew," said Gloria.

The next day about noon Robin was wandering restlessly about the castle. He wanted to go riding, but the Princess hadn't come from her room yet, and he felt that it would be impolite to go off without inviting her to go with him. He went up to the second floor where her rooms were, hoping to catch sight of one of her servants and find out whether she was likely to appear very soon.

He saw the little purple maid coming down the hall with a large tray of food for the Princess. "Good morning," he said.

She started violently at sight of him, and dropped the tray, scattering food and dishes everywhere.

Robin said, "Oh, I'm sorry I startled you. Let me help you pick them up."

The little purple maid only put her hands to her face and sank to the floor trembling and sobbing silently.

"It's all right," Robin said, distressed. "It doesn't matter. Run and get another tray, and send one of the servants to clear this away."

But the little maid only shuddered, and started picking the dishes up in a great hurry. Robin couldn't understand why she should be so frightened. But he was sorry he had been the cause of it, so he decided to go down himself and tell them to prepare another breakfast for the Princess Bluebell. He did so, and then came back upstairs to see if the little maid was all right.

The stairs and halls were thickly carpeted, so when

Robin came back the two people in the hall didn't hear him. As he reached the top of the stairs he heard the Princess's voice.

"You ugly, clumsy, purple thing!" she was saying furiously. "You're five minutes late with my breakfast! If you're not careful, something worse will happen to you!" She slapped the little purple maid as hard as she could. The little maid didn't say anything, but just stood there, swaying a little.

"Look here, it wasn't her fault," Robin said, walking up to them quickly. "I scared her. She didn't see me, and dropped the tray. I've already sent for another for you, Princess."

The Princess was all smiles. "Oh, I'm sure it couldn't have been your fault," she said sweetly. "She's *very* stupid, you know. No one else would put up with her, but I keep her because I'm sorry for her."

The little maid shivered.

Robin thought he'd better change the subject, so he asked the Princess if she'd like to ride with him.

"No, thank you," she said. "I'm a little tired today. We did dance so very late last night. You go on, Robin. I don't want you to stay at home on my account."

Robin certainly didn't want to stay at home on her account. He got Mika to go with him, and they rode out across the valley together.

"I don't think I can possibly marry the Princess Bluebell," Robin said as the horses ambled along.

"We don't want you to marry anyone you don't want

to marry," Mika said. "I don't know that I'm sorry. I don't think I could ever be very fond of her."

"She slapped that little maid of hers this morning for something that was an accident," Robin said. "I think her sweet disposition has been overrated."

"Hmmmm," said Mika. "A true princess is never cruel to her servants, and never unladylike."

"The things she said were not very ladylike," Robin said. "Do you have to invite another princess? It's not much fun, you know, having a girl brought to visit, and then knowing everyone is watching to see whether you fall in love with her or not."

"I know," said Mika. "Anyway, Princess Bluebell is still here, and we certainly can't invite another until she's gone."

"When is she going?"

"I don't know. She hasn't said anything at all about the length of her visit. *She* seems to like *you*."

Robin just growled under his breath.

CHAPTER 5

Something Wrong

SIMPLY DON'T LIKE THAT PRIN-
cess Bluebell," Robin said that night to Gloria.

"I—I'm afraid I don't like her either," Gloria said.
"But she's very beautiful."

"Her face is all right, I guess. But I don't like *her*.
Can't you get her to go away?"

"I can't order her to leave, Robin. It wouldn't be polite, and besides, her father is a powerful king. These fairies are so touchy. Sometimes I think they make war just
for the fun of it."

They were giving a small dinner party for the Princess
that night, and Gloria and Robin went down together.
Flumpdoria was there, and three of Mika's brothers and
their wives, and a few others. There was also Wuddle, a
prince of the Swamp Fairies, damp and green and
slithery.

No one seemed to have a very good time, except Bluebell. After dinner there was dancing, and her gay laugh could be heard frequently as she danced with one partner and then another.

Robin danced with her a few times, but stood in a corner most of the time, adding nothing to the gaiety of the occasion.

Flumpdoria came up to him and said, "What's the matter with you, Robin? You don't have to marry the girl, you know."

"She gets on my nerves," he said grumpily. "She gives me the creeps."

Flumpdoria looked thoughtful. "She certainly isn't much like the description of her we had before she came. I'm going to ask our ambassador to the Blue Elves where he got the idea he was a judge of princesses."

"I'd like to talk to him, too."

"He'll be here for the Grand Ball Thursday night. Why do you suppose Mika and Gloria invited that ugly Swamp Prince, Wuddle?"

"When we were out riding today," Robin said, "we met him, and he practically invited himself. Father said he had once been the cause of a war with the Swamp Fairies, and didn't want to start any more trouble, so he told him to come."

"That was when Mika refused to marry a Swamp Princess, Prince Wuddle's sister," Flumpdoria told him. "I heard Prince Wuddle wanted to marry Princess Bluebell, and she wouldn't have him. Maybe he came here to see her."

"He can have her," Robin said. He kept thinking of how the Princess had treated her maid.

Then he thought of the things Tinkle had said, or had refused to say, and decided to slip away and see if he could find out what was wrong. He told Flumpdoria where he was going, and went out to the servants' hall.

He watched the servants for a moment as they went busily to and fro, before they saw him. All the castle servants had rather anxious expressions on their faces, and kept glancing uneasily at the servants Princess Bluebell had brought with her. These were sitting in a group by themselves, doing nothing, and talking in whispers.

Away over in a corner sat the little maid, huddled away from everyone.

Then they saw him, and all the castle servants gathered around Robin and curtsied or bowed, and asked if there was anything they could do for him.

"Is anything wrong?" he asked. "Why is everyone so nervous? I want to know."

They all looked frightened, but no one spoke.

"Meeky, you tell me," he said impatiently.

Meeky was the head cook. She looked around as though she wanted to run away.

"I—I don't know, Master Robin—I mean Your Highness. There *is* something, only we don't know what. Things go wrong. Everybody's on edge. You'd almost think there were goblins about."

She looked darkly across the room. The other servants followed her gaze. They were looking at the Princess

5 4

Bluebell's servants, and particularly at the ugly little maid. She looked forlorn and frightened and sad.

"Do you think she really can't speak?" Meeky asked.

"I don't know," Robin said, and walked over to where the little maid was sitting. She stood up and curtsied.

"Is anything the matter?" Robin asked kindly.

The little maid shook her head.

"Can you understand what I'm saying?"

She nodded.

"Can't you speak?"

She shook her head again.

"Can you read and write?"

She shook her head, and Robin gave up. There was nothing to be learned from her.

He asked the Princess's servants if they had noticed anything wrong, and they grinned and said no. Somehow Robin didn't like them. Their words were respectful, but their manner was faintly mocking. He felt sorry for the little purple maid, but he disliked the Princess's other servants.

He told his own servants to try not to get upset over nothing, and went back to the ballroom and danced with the Princess.

She talked vivaciously, and told him how much she was enjoying her visit, and how she hated to think of going home again.

Robin said, "Must you go home?" politely, but he couldn't put much regret into his voice. The Princess said she didn't have to go quite yet, and wouldn't the Grand

Ball next Thursday be a wonderful occasion, and wasn't he looking forward to it?

Robin thought that what he was looking forward to was talking to the ambassador to the Blue Elves. He was going to tell him that he'd better use some of his diplomacy and get Princess Bluebell to go back where she came from.

He was glad when the dance was over and another partner claimed the Princess. Somehow he just didn't like to dance with her. He didn't like to take her hand. She made him feel creepy.

Oh, well, it was probably his imagination.

He went outdoors, and walked in the garden, and talked to the fairies. They always came and looked on whenever there was a party. They were the fairies who took care of the little animals in the woods, and the fairies who opened the buds of the flowers, and the elves who made boots and beautiful clothes for the royal family.

They crowded around him, the little things, and told him how glad they were to see him, and asked when Meira was coming home. They asked him if he needed a new pair of boots, and if he'd like to see some very new rabbits.

With the fairies fluttering about him or perched on his shoulders, he walked a little way up the mountain into the woods, just to take a peek at the very new rabbits.

After a little while he turned and started back toward the castle. When he came to it he stopped and gazed a moment.

It stood, a huge pile of stone, black against the sky. Robin had seen his home thus many times before, but tonight it made him feel uneasy.

The castle seemed grim and forbidding, sad and menacing at the same time, as though something hid there, watching.

"What is it?" Robin said at last, softly. "Do you know what it is?"

The fairies fluttered about and whispered, "No. We don't know . . . we don't know . . ."

Robin hurried back to the castle and came into the ballroom. The guests were beginning to leave rather early. Usually they danced until dawn. But after the first guest had made his farewells, the others followed quickly. They seemed glad to go.

Flumpdoria was the last to leave. "Good night," she said, and paused. She stood a moment in thoughtful silence. "If you need me . . ." she began, and stopped again. "Maybe it's my imagination. . . ."

"No, it isn't," Robin said.

"You felt it too?" Mika asked. "I wasn't going to say anything, but. . . ."

"Well, you call me if you want to," Flumpdoria said. "I really have some important work to do, or I'd stay and see what all this is about."

After she had gone, Mika went upstairs with Gloria.

"It wasn't a very good party, was it?" he said.

"No," Gloria said. "Everybody's so jumpy, and Robin goes around looking just the way I feel. I'm afraid the poor boy thinks we want him to marry that dreadful princess."

"No, he doesn't. I told him so. Everyone seems to think that little purple maid is causing the trouble, although I must say she seems harmless enough to me. Now, go to sleep, Gloria."

In the meantime, Robin had gone to his room, and was sitting on the wide stone window sill looking out into the garden. The castle had become quiet, and everyone was asleep.

Then he saw something in the garden. The moon was bright, and two people were there, walking about and talking. They stayed in the shadows of the trees most of the time, but once they walked through a patch of bright moonlight, and he saw that they were the Princess Bluebell and Wuddle, the Swamp Prince.

"I wonder what they're talking about so late at night?" he thought.

In a few minutes they parted. Prince Wuddle slipped silently away, and the Princess came back to the castle. Robin continued to sit by the window for a long time, thinking.

Maybe there *was* some danger. Living so near the goblin country, it was possible, though they had never had any trouble with them before. He decided to look through the castle. He went downstairs and spoke to the guard at the main door.

"Look around," Robin said. "I think there may be goblins about. I'm not sure, but see if you can find anything suspicious."

"Yes, Your Highness," the guard said. "But I don't see how any goblins could get in."

Robin prowled through the castle, gloomy in the night. Once he thought he heard a noise, but it wasn't repeated.

Still he felt uneasy, and couldn't help wondering what the Princess Bluebell had been doing, slipping out to talk to the Swamp Prince in the middle of the night.

Suddenly he decided what he was going to do. He ran downstairs and out of the castle, going quickly to the magic rock, the same one that Gloria had sat on when she first came to the enchanted valley, while she waited for Mika to come back from Fairyland.

Robin stood with his hand on the rock, and said the magic spell beginning: "Ebbledum, wex, gomple be-doop . . ." and so on.

Immediately he found himself transported within the borders of Fairyland. Hurriedly he made his way to Flumpdoria's house. She was astonished to see him in the middle of the night, but roused herself quickly to hear what he had to say. They talked a long time, and then Flumpdoria said,

"I'll do what I can, boy. But Glauz is in his yearly trance and it's impossible to wake him. Goblin dust is very hard to make, you know. There are only a few grains in the kingdom. I can't possibly get you any before the night of the Grand Ball."

"I'll just hope that that will be in time," Robin said. "Of course, I may be all wrong, but I'll depend on you for Thursday, anyway. Good-by, and thanks tremendously."

He hurried away, and was in the castle and in his room again before anyone waked up.

He was glad he had consulted his godmother. (Flumpdoria was his godmother, too.) He would feel safer with some goblin dust in the house. One grain of it on goblins' skin is so painful that they become frantic, and cannot do anything until they have covered themselves with butter; and goblins have very little butter. But goblin dust is made only by the finest magicians and is very scarce. It was an unhandy time for Glauz to be in his yearly trance.

The next day Mika and Gloria were puzzled, because while everyone else was depressed and gloomy—except the Princess—Robin seemed almost cheerful.

And he was *very* attentive to the Princess Bluebell.

"I can't understand it," Gloria said. "Do you think he's falling in love with her after all?"

"I hardly think so," Mika said.

Mika didn't get a chance to ask him, though, because Robin was always with the Princess Bluebell. He was with her every moment of the day, and danced with her constantly that night after dinner.

The Princess seemed to like this very much, and told Gloria how handsome her son was, and how she liked staying at the castle with them.

"I could hardly be polite," Gloria told Mika later. "I usually like everyone, but I wish Robin wouldn't stay with her so much."

"He's up to something," Mika said.

CHAPTER 6

Robin Stirs Up Trouble

THURSDAY, THE DAY OF THE Grand Ball, the Princess Bluebell stayed in her rooms all day, trying on gowns for the ball. She said she just couldn't decide what to wear.

The little purple maid could be seen frequently, all day long, running upstairs and downstairs in a great hurry, on errands for her mistress.

At last the time for the great occasion arrived, and all the guests were assembling in the great ballroom. Mika came in with the guest of honor, Princess Bluebell, on his arm, and Gloria came in with her son Robin.

The Princess's gown was the blue of the sea, with changing lights in it, and decorated with tiny pearls, and crystals from the Blue Crystal Caves of Blue Elfland.

Gloria was clothed all in clinging white, and her golden

hair shone like the sun. A girdle of purple flowers was about her waist, and a circlet of flowers in her hair.

This Grand Ball was a great occasion. It was given once a year at the castle. All the royal families of all the fairy kingdoms were invited, and the people of their courts. The Fire Fairies were there, the Blue Elves, the River Fairies, the Snow Fairies, the Flower Fairies, and many others. The Swamp Fairies were invited, too, although no one wanted them very much. They looked disagreeable and never seemed to be enjoying themselves, but they always came. There were so many guests that the great ballroom could hardly hold them, and the whole first floor of the castle was thrown open.

Intricate dances were performed, with names like the Royal Circle, Stars in Iceland, Twilight Minuet, and many others.

Before the dancing began, however, everyone walked about and watched the new arrivals as they were announced by the heralds with their silver trumpets.

Robin sought out the ambassador to Blue Elfland, whose name was Zeret, and after the usual polite greetings, he said:

"Is the Princess Bluebell your choice of all the princesses in Fairyland?"

"I—er—Your Highness," Zeret said, looking worried, and then stopped. "She—she doesn't seem . . ." He stopped again.

"Doesn't seem what?"

"She doesn't seem the same. She looks just the same. I can't tell how she's different, but she *is*."

"What do you mean?"

"Look at her father and mother," said Zeret. "Look at all the people from the court of the Blue Elves."

Robin looked, and saw that the King and Queen of the Blue Elves and all the people from Blue Elfland were standing together, looking in the same direction, just standing there, instead of mingling with the other guests. They were gazing at the Princess Bluebell, who was walking about the room with Mika.

And on the face of every one of them Robin saw the same expression of doubt and puzzlement.

"Her own people," Zeret was saying. "They notice it. I tell you she's changed. I don't know how, but she is."

"I see," said Robin. "Don't worry." He turned away and wandered through the crowd of guests, trying to behave as he was expected to, and looking toward the door every few minutes.

Why didn't Flumpdoria come? She was very late. Then he heard the trumpets of the heralds, and his godmother was announced.

Robin hardly gave her time to greet all the kings and queens and say the polite things she was supposed to say. At last she excused herself, and Robin grasped her arm.

"Flumpy!" he said, leading her away from the ballroom to a quiet spot where they could talk. "Did you . . . ?"

"Yes, yes, child. Stop pulling at me. I look bad enough already. I had to hurry so to get here. Here. If you knew the trouble I had getting this. . . ."

"Thanks so much," Robin interrupted her. "What's the first dance? The Royal Circle?"

"Yes." Flumpdoria handed him a queer-looking ring with a large green stone in it. He slipped it on his finger.

"I'm going to do it then. Be watching, Flumpy. Things are likely to happen."

"I should say so. Well, go on, child, and get it over with."

Robin came back into the great ballroom just as the Royal Circle was announced.

The Princess Bluebell was his partner, and he went and took her hand as the beautiful and unearthly music of the fairy orchestra began. They danced and turned and whirled, and as the dance went on Robin became so nervous that he almost forgot one of the steps. "There's no use putting it off," he said to himself. "I must do it now."

The partners dropped hands and turned about slowly. As he turned away from the Princess, Robin pressed a catch in the ring, and the top of the green stone opened. He took something out of the ring quickly and snapped it shut again, as he turned back toward the Princess.

The partners all joined hands again, and as he touched the hand of the Princess Bluebell, Robin dropped a tiny grain of sand into it.

Immediately there was a tremendous flash of red light and the most awful screams. Robin was blinded for a moment by the bright light, and when he could see again, the Princess Bluebell had disappeared.

Dancers stopped dancing and rushed about, calling to each other, wanting to know what the matter was.

65

And all the time terrible screams were going on, louder and louder, and a frantic, ugly, horrible green creature ran and shoved and pushed at the crowd of guests, trying to get out.

"Butter! *Butter!* BUTTER!" it screamed. "Eeeeee! Oooooh! Butter! *Butter!*"

The guests stepped aside quickly to let it through, and it ran out of the room, still screaming, and out of the castle, screaming, screaming, and everyone stood still and listened as the awful sounds died away in the distance, becoming fainter and fainter until they could be heard no more.

Then a long, shuddering, whispered sigh went up from all the dancers, and from all the castle. Everything was quite still, until Gloria said in a whisper, "Where did that come from?"

"That," said Robin, wiping his brow with a handkerchief, made of the finest cobwebs, "was the Princess Bluebell."

Then everyone started talking at once, and the ones who had been too far away to see anything were asking what had happened. Robin explained to the ones nearest him, and they told the ones next to them, and in a few minutes the entire company knew that Robin had put a grain of goblin dust in the Princess Bluebell's hand, and that she had turned into a goblin!

Robin was standing near the door into the hall where the stair was, which led to the upper stories. He happened to glance out into the hall, and saw—a goblin!

Then another slipped past the door, and another! At

66

the same time there was a frightful uproar from the servants' hall, shouts and cries and sounds of running feet.

"What's that?" Mika cried, and rushed to see what was the matter, the guests crowding after him. Robin started to go too, and then stopped. Where had those goblins in the hall come from? How could they have got into the castle?

He ran out into the hall. There, a dozen or more goblins were running toward the servants' hall, where the noise of fighting was growing louder and louder.

He ran toward them. They seemed to be coming from a small room halfway down the hall, a room that wasn't used very much. Knocking goblins aside he rushed into this room, and saw that a window was open, and goblins were pouring in through it. He rushed over to the window, saying the spell that had been put on all the windows in the castle, the spell that kept goblins from ever coming in whether the windows were open or shut. Someone was taking the spells off the windows.

He heard a sound in a room adjoining and ran in there. And there was the Swamp Prince, Wuddle! He was waving a wand in front of a window, saying an incantation and removing the invisible barrier that had kept the inhabitants of the castle safe for so many years!

Robin ran and grasped his arm before he could finish the disenchantment, but just then a goblin ran up and attacked him, almost making him lose his balance, and Prince Wuddle was very damp and slippery. He gave a sudden jerk and wrenched himself away, running out of the room, with Robin behind him.

He simply had to stop him. If the castle should be over-come by the goblin hordes, the disaster would be awful. All the kings of all the fairy kingdoms were there, and if these should all be captured, all Fairyland might be over-thrown completely.

Prince Wuddle ran toward the servants' hall, with Robin tearing along behind him, and dashed through the door.

Robin burst in right after him, but lost sight of him in the confusion. All the castle servants, with brooms and mops, or any weapons they could find, and many of the guests, were fighting furiously with dozens of goblins.

He couldn't see Prince Wuddle anywhere in the crowd, but he noticed a startling thing.

The Swamp Fairies were fighting on the side of the goblins!

CHAPTER 7

The Mystery Explained

HEN ROBIN WHIRLED ABOUT AS
he heard a woman scream, and was just in time to see
Prince Wuddle dragging a girl through the window, out
into the castle grounds. For an instant beautiful implor-
ing eyes were turned toward Robin, then the green arms
of the Swamp Prince encircled her, and she disappeared
into the night.

Robin ran to the window and leaped through it onto the
ground. He saw two struggling forms going through the
moonlight, and ran after them.

Prince Wuddle was running as fast as he could, dragging the girl, who was doing her best to pull him the other
way. Robin could go much faster, of course, and soon
caught up with them.

He leaped at Prince Wuddle, dragging him to the
ground, and causing him to loose his hold on his captive.

The Swamp Fairy wriggled and squirmed, and they rolled and trumbled on the ground. Wuddle got his hands on a large stone and brought it down with all his force on Robin's head.

The shock was so great that Robin's senses reeled, but he tightened his arms about Wuddle's waist and held on for dear life. Wuddle raised the stone to hit him again, but the girl stepped up and caught his arm, and snatched the stone from him.

Robin was weak and dizzy from the blow and was afraid that, if he let go to try to get a better hold on him, Wuddle would get away entirely. The girl was still holding Wuddle's arm, and he shook her back and forth as he struggled to get free.

Then, with a mighty heave, Robin sat up suddenly, and his fist crashed into Wuddle's jaw. The Swamp Prince lay panting weakly, and Robin stood up with an effort. Wuddle struggled to his feet, and Robin hit him again, knocking him senseless.

He took him by the collar and dragged him toward the castle.

"Come on," he said to the girl.

"Oh, Robin!" she said, and put her arm around his waist to help him walk, as he feebly dragged the heavy Wuddle along.

They came thus into the great hall, in which only the women guests were left. All the men were fighting goblins in the back of the castle.

The women rushed over to him, and Robin said wearily,

"Go and get someone to take charge of this, please." He dumped Wuddle on the floor and sat on him.

Flumpdoria hurried out, and soon came back with two of Mika's brothers, who picked Prince Wuddle up and carried him away to lock him up in the dungeon below the castle.

"The fighting's almost over," Flumpdoria said. "They've captured a great many, and locked them up in the dungeon. Some of the cowardly things ran away, and I think we'll soon subdue the ones who are left. You wait here until I come back."

Robin felt no desire to move. His head was throbbing painfully and he felt very sick. He sat there thinking that things might have turned out very differently if Wuddle had succeeded in opening the whole castle to the hordes of goblins who were waiting for a chance to get in.

In a few minutes Flumpdoria was back again. She had been to the medicine chest and brought some soothing fairy ointment for goblin scratches, and something else that she had rubbed on Robin's forehead, and his headache disappeared in a few minutes.

Feeling well again, Robin hurried out to help the others with the captives. He passed groups of fairies dragging goblins and Swamp Fairies toward the dungeons.

In the servants' hall they were chasing six goblins and a Swamp Fairy around and around. At last they caught two of the goblins, and the others managed to slip away through the window.

Those injured in the fight were lying all about on the

floor, and Robin called to Flumpdoria to come and bring the healing ointment.

Some of them were badly hurt, and there was no one who hadn't at least a scratch or two, and, as goblin scratches are poison, they had to be attended to at once.

Robin searched for the girl who had helped him in his fight with Wuddle. He had been so busy fighting that he had hardly looked at her.

He found her at last, with her head on the shoulder of the Queen of the Blue Elves, crying. When Robin appeared, she looked up. There could be no doubt about it.

She was the Princess Bluebell, the *real* Princess Bluebell.

"Darling," her mother was saying soothingly, "you must stop crying and tell us what happened."

The Princess dried her eyes. Robin could not take his eyes from her. She was dressed in the ugly clothes of the little purple maid, and her face was streaked with tears, but there was no doubt that here was the real Princess. A gentle light shone in her blue eyes, and one could tell that she would never be cruel to anything. The face of the other princess, so like hers, seemed now like a mask. Though the features were exactly the same, no one could believe that he had been deceived by the other princess.

People crowded around her to hear what she had to say.

"About halfway between here and my own country," the Princess said, "my coach was suddenly surrounded by goblins. Before we knew what had happened, a powerful spell was laid upon us.

"I looked out of the window, and there I saw—myself!

And then I looked into my little mirror and saw that I had been changed into a most ugly purple creature. I was terribly frightened.

"This girl who looked like me touched my footmen and all my escort with a wand, and they were turned into a line of stones along the road. And the goblins changed, and became like my servants who had come with me.

"It was a very powerful spell, for none of us could move or do anything except what we were told. The goblin princess made me change clothes with her, and told me I couldn't talk or write or read, and I couldn't. They got into the coach, and on the horses, and left all of us but me lying on the ground changed into stones.

"The goblin princess took me with her, and said I was to be her maid. All this time I have had to serve her, and everyone hated me, and I couldn't speak. Oooooh!" The Princess began to cry again.

"If Robin hadn't found her out," Mika said, "Wuddle would have filled the castle with goblins before we knew there was anything wrong at all."

The Princess shuddered. "It was a plan to overthrow all the fairy kingdoms," she said. "She is the daughter of the goblin king. She and Prince Wuddle met every night, planning how to do it."

"I saw them once," Robin said.

"She was always telling me how the goblins were going to rule over all Fairyland. Prince Wuddle had been trying to get me to marry him, but I would have nothing to do with him. So he agreed to get his people to help the goblins if she'd give me to him as his wife."

"I see," Flumpdoria said. "The Swamp Fairies are half goblin anyway, and they've never been very friendly."

"But how did you know, Robin?" the guests were saying. "You had never seen the Princess Bluebell before."

"She made me feel creepy," Robin said. "I didn't like to touch her. And then I saw her slipping out in the night, and everyone in the castle was nervous and uneasy, and I was almost sure it was because goblins were about. The servants didn't trust the little maid, but it was the Princess who made me feel queer.

"So I asked Flumpdoria for some goblin dust. If she had been the real princess she wouldn't even have noticed the grain of dust I put into her hand, so no harm would have been done."

"I hope you've been careful with that dust," Flumpdoria said. "It takes years to make a single grain, and it's our best protection against them."

Robin gave her back the ring. "I used only one grain," he said.

"The goblin dust broke the spell," Bluebell said. "We were all in the servants' hall, and suddenly I heard those awful screams, and all the goblins who had been changed to look like my servants turned into goblins again, and everyone started fighting. I looked down at myself and I wasn't purple any more. Then you all ran in from the ballroom, and before I knew it, Wuddle had dragged me through the window."

The guests all started talking at once, exclaiming over their narrow escape. They were trying to decide what to do with the captives when the great magician Glauz suddenly appeared, looking rather sleepy.

"What's been going on?" he asked. "You've disturbed my trance, with so much magic crackling in the air."

They told him what had happened and Glauz said he would dispose of the captured goblins and Swamp Fairies. He waved his wand, and said, "Look at the door handles."

They all went over to the doors and looked and saw that all the handles were now goblin or Swamp Fairy heads. "The rest of them's inside the door," Glauz said, and yawned and disappeared.

Later on when Glauz woke from the trance the battle had interrupted, he told them that the goblins would stay imprisoned in the doors of the castle so long as it should stand, and would not be so anxious to get into mischief when they were finally released.

They never did find out how Prince Wuddle had discovered a spell to let the goblins in through the windows.

As they had captured the King of the Swamp Fairies, and Prince Wuddle and a great many others, they didn't have much to fear from the Swamp Fairies for some time, for all their leaders were gone.

CHAPTER 8

Robin and Bluebell

WHILE EVERYONE WAS TALKING about the fight, Gloria and the Queen of the Blue Elves took Princess Bluebell upstairs. They wanted her to rest, but she wouldn't think of it.

"I feel so happy at being myself again," she said, "that I want to dance all night. I hope I can find a decent gown that the goblin princess hasn't worn. I couldn't *bear* to wear anything she's had on."

They looked over the Princess's clothes, and found many gowns the goblin princess hadn't worn.

"She used all my prettiest ones," Bluebell sighed.

Downstairs the guests were saying that perhaps they'd better go home, as the Princess would want to rest after her terrible experience.

"Rest nothing!" Flumpdoria said. "Look."

There was the Princess Bluebell coming across the

floor, looking ten times as beautiful as the goblin princess had looked, even with the same face.

They decided to start the ball all over again and asked the Princess with whom she wanted to dance. She said she'd like to have Robin for her partner, because he had been so nice to her even when she was purple and ugly.

Robin was very pleased and embarrassed at this, as he took her hand for the Royal Circle.

All evening Robin and Bluebell hardly took their eyes away from each other, and they didn't seem to want to dance with anyone else.

"I suppose you see what's happening," Flumpdoria said to Mika.

"Hmmmph. What?" said Mika.

"They're falling in love, that's what," Flumpdoria said. "So you can start worrying about something else."

Before the ball was over, it was proved that Flumpdoria was right, for Robin asked the Princess to marry him, and she agreed.

It was love at first sight with Robin, but probably the Princess Bluebell had been in love with him all the time she had been at the castle, although she wouldn't say so, of course.

She said that anyway she knew Robin hadn't fallen in love with her for her beauty alone, because he had seen it for so long in the face of the goblin princess.

Robin said that the goblin princess hadn't looked a thing in the world like his Bluebell, and no one could convince him that she had.

He was very impatient, and said what was the use of

letting all these people go home, when they'd have to come back so soon for the wedding. King Klux said he didn't care how soon it was. The King and Queen of the Blue Elves said it was very sudden, and what about a trousseau, and Bluebell was awfully young, and so forth.

But Robin and Bluebell persuaded them, and the wedding was set for a week from that night.

The fairy goldsmiths and cobblers and dressmakers started working like mad, setting jewels and making slippers, and the most beautiful clothes from moonbeams and mist, dewdrops, cobwebs fine spun, rainbows, and many other rare and lovely materials. There was must bustling about in the castle, and all the guests stayed and rejoiced for the whole week, getting dreadfully in the way at times, but everyone was so happy they didn't mind at all.

Gloria was very busy, so Mika went to Kengaria to tell King Ferdinand and Queen Katrina and Meira, and bring them back for the wedding. He took a special magic chariot, and in no time at all he was in Kengaria.

Queen Katrina jumped nervously as he appeared in the dining hall while they were having dinner. Meira ran and threw her arms around him.

"Oh, Daddy darling! I'm so glad to see you!"

"We're very glad indeed to see you, Mika," King Ferdinand said. "But I do wish you wouldn't appear so suddenly. It frets the Queen."

"I'm all right now," Queen Katrina said. "You did give me a turn, though."

"I have some news for you," Mika said. "Robin is going to be married."

"Robin! Married!" Then there were excited questions, and Mika told them the whole story of the Princess Blue-bell, and the things that had been happening at the castle.

Queen Katrina said it sounded like indecent haste to her, but that young people nowadays never would let themselves be crossed, and that Mika was as bad as Robin.

"Consider, my dear," said King Ferdinand. "Mika is several hundred years older than you are yourself."

Queen Katrina looked at Mika, who of course seemed to be a very young man, for fairies age very slowly.

"Impossible!" she said, and as far as she was concerned, that was that.

"I must order a new gown this minute," Meira said. "I do hope I shall like Bluebell."

"You'll love her," Mika said. "But the fairies will be terribly hurt if you don't wear the one they're making for you."

"Oh, of course!" Meira said. "It will be much nicer than anything I can get here."

The Queen sniffed. "You won't get me into any of those magic garments," she said. "Likely to disappear at the stroke of twelve, or something!"

Mika laughed, and said to wear anything she wanted to.

"I wonder if they're making me a new robe or any-thing," King Ferdinand said wistfully. The King had a nice taste in clothes, and considered the fairies' workman-ship finer than anything he could get in his own country.

"Of course," said Mika. "Wait till you see it." He was very fond of his father-in-law, and if the fairies hadn't thought of making him a robe for the wedding, Mika was going to see that he got one, if he had to make it himself.

After two days they were ready, and Mika put them all into the magic chariot and took them to the enchanted valley.

Bluebell and Robin had a beautiful wedding, and the guests overflowed the castle, and camped in lovely silk tents all over the valley. Every fairy from every kingdom was invited. Of course they couldn't *all* come, but it was the largest wedding ever seen up to that time.

"There doesn't seem to be much difficulty about their marrying each other," Gloria said, thinking of how she and Mika had been married, and how furious King Klux had been.

"Of course not," said Flumpdoria. "Robin has to be one thing or the other, officially anyway. He can't just go along being half fairy and half mortal."

"But he is," Gloria protested.

"If he marries a fairy, he has to be a fairy. It's the law," Flumpdoria explained. "If he had married a mortal, he'd be a mortal, to all intents and purposes."

And that was all she would say about it.

Mika and Gloria asked Robin and Bluebell to live in the castle with them after they were married, and they decided that would be nice, so they did.

"And lived happy ever after?" Lucy asked.

"Yes," said Michael. "They were very happy indeed."

"And did the Princess Meira live there, too, or did she go back to Kengaria?"

"That's another story," said Michael, and he sat so silent for so long that the air began to be purple again.

The shadows darkened again as soon as he stopped talking, and there was no sound, except for the very faintest whispering and rustling.

Flumpdoria began to sniff at Lucy's lunch basket, so she opened it, and they each had two sandwiches apiece while Michael began to tell her about the Princess Meira.

CHAPTER 9

Meira

WHICH ONE IS MEIRA'S SHADOW?"
Lucy asked softly.

"It isn't there," Michael said after a moment. "You see, Meira is not in Fairyland."

"She *isn't?*"

No (Michael told her). After Robin and Bluebell were married they lived in the castle with Mika and Gloria, and Meira was there too, but she was very restless. She loved the fairies, but she never could feel like one of them. And she liked mortals, but she just couldn't feel like one of them either.

After a time she decided to go back to Kengaria and visit her grandmother and grandfather, who were very glad indeed to have her.

Meira had a wonderful time, going to balls and being

courted by many youths who admired the beautiful princess. There were two young men who were particularly persistent in their efforts to get her to marry them— Prince Johann, Crown Prince of a neighboring kingdom, and young Count Frederik of Frippen, a noble of Kengaria. Meira enjoyed having the two young men argue about her, and had no intention of choosing between them at all.

But soon she began to be restless again, because she wasn't all mortal, either, and began to spend a good deal of time on the palace roof, where she could be alone. She would stand and gaze over the parapets at a beautiful mountain that could be seen in the distance. It looked quite blue at its base, and about halfway up there was always a ring of cloud, through which the summit of the mountain rose, as pink as could be.

Its name was the Mount of the Dragons, and the people of Kengaria were afraid to go there, although everyone knew that there were no dragons in the land any more.

"Some day I shall go there," Meira told herself.

When she tired of looking at the mountain, she began taking long rides about the countryside on her pony, slipping away so no one would go with her. Frederik and Johann spent most of their time looking for her.

One day as she was riding she crossed a shallow stream; she was wearing a cap with a feather in it, and a sudden gust of wind lifted it in the air and dropped it in the water. Meira was leaning over, trying to reach it from her pony's back, when she heard the sound of horse's hooves, and a young man rode up, and leaning down, picked the cap out of the water with no trouble at all.

"Thank you so much," Meira said. "I don't think I could have reached it."

The young man laid the cap on a rock in the sun to dry, and they both dismounted and sat down on the rock, too.

"My name is Julian," the young man said, smiling at her. His gray eyes were merry, and he seemed to be in a very good humor. The sun glinted in his curly brown hair when he took off his hat.

"I am Meira, granddaughter of King Ferdinand," said Meira.

"The Princess Meira," said Julian, standing up and bowing. "I have heard she's very beautiful, and doesn't know what she wants. The first part is certainly true," he added, sitting down again.

"Thank you," said Meira. "The other is true, too. I just can't decide what I am. Fairies are so much like fairies, and mortals are so much like mortals, and I don't seem to be either one."

"Ah," he said. "That's your trouble. You mustn't try to be either, when really you're a third kind of person."

"Perhaps you're right," she said. "I'll try it. I suppose I'd better go now. It's getting late, and no one knows where I am."

Julian rode part of the way with her to the palace, until they came to a fork in the road, when he swept off his plumed hat and said that perhaps they would meet again.

Meira watched him as he rode off, whistling cheerily, and after that she thought about Julian a good deal, and wondered where he lived, and who he was. She rode often, watching for a sight of him, but several weeks passed, and she didn't see him again. She began to feel very sad.

"It can't be because of Julian," she told herself. "After all, I've seen him only once. I wish I had something to do."

Then she thought of the Mount of the Dragons. "I'll go there tomorrow!" she decided.

The next morning she got up very early and rode away gaily through the crisp, morning air, her pony's hooves scattering dew drops as he cantered along.

After a long while she reached the mountain, and saw that a path zigzagged up its side. As her pony began to climb, she noticed that little blue flowers poked their heads from the grass, more and more of them as she went along, until at last there wasn't any grass and she was riding through a thick carpet of blue flowers.

After a while the path began to wind round and round the mountain, and she noticed that the air was cooler, and that there was a slight mist. This mist grew thicker and thicker until she could see only a little bit ahead of her. The flowers on the ground now appeared to be a light purple.

"I'm riding right through the ring of cloud I saw from the palace," she thought. The air became cooler and the mist thicker, until she couldn't see anything, and sat there shivering while her pony picked his way along.

Then, just as she was beginning to be a little frightened, they suddenly came out of the cloud into the bright sunshine. And now they were going over a carpet of pink flowers, growing very thickly. Her clothes and the pony's hide glistened with a dewiness that had settled on them from the mist, but this moisture soon disappeared in the sun. The path began to zigzag again, steeply, and then—they were at the top.

Lovely level fields of pink flowers stretched away, with trees here and there covered with pink or white blossoms. Against the blue sky, it was almost too lovely to believe.

The path led away to the left, through two rows of fruit trees. She saw, somewhat startled, that the trees were in bloom and had fruit on them at the same time. The mountain must be enchanted. But Meira had always been used to enchantments of one kind or another so it didn't bother her much.

The path ended suddenly, in front of a rounded hill, and set into this hill was a perfectly huge blue door, with gold hinges.

Meira jumped to the ground. Probably she should leave it alone, but she just had to see what was behind that door. After all, no one had lived here for centuries. The door was so large that she could just barely reach the handle, but when she pulled at it, it opened easily. She peeped in.

There was an immense room, hollowed out of the inside of the hill. The walls were hung with rich tapestries and furnished with huge divans and mushroom-like hassocks almost as tall as she was. From a round skylight in the top, light streamed in, and the floor was covered with lovely purple flowers like the ones that grew in the mist. Meira roamed about in delight, thinking that whoever had lived here must have been very large.

Then she heard a loud, frightened neigh, and the galloping of hooves. She rushed to the door.

Her pony was almost out of sight, racing in terror down the mountain, and there, right in front of her, was a *very* large dragon.

Meira couldn't speak or move. She just stood there, staring up at the monster in trembling horror. She closed her eyes.

"Don't be afraid," the dragon said in a soft voice. "I won't hurt you. I'm a vegetarian," he added.

Meira leaned against the door weakly. He really didn't look very fierce. There was an anxious expression on his face.

"I hope I didn't startle you too much," he said. "You see, I didn't know you were here."

"I certainly didn't know *you* were here," Meira said, "or I never should have come."

"I'm very glad you did," said the dragon. "I get so lonely."

"Aren't there any other dragons?"

"No," he said sadly, "not for miles. And I just can't leave my mountain to go and live with them."

"Why not?" asked Meira.

"Why, because I live *here*. I like it. But it's very lonely."

"I can see that it would be," she said. "What's your name? I am Meira, granddaughter of King Ferdinand."

The dragon made a low obeisance. "I am called Branstookah."

"How do you do? Tell me," Meira said, "how have you

lived here so long without anyone knowing about you?"

"I can't let any humans know. They all think dragons eat people, and there'd be armies up here, trying to kill me."

"What a shame! But couldn't you tell them you wouldn't hurt them?"

"Tell them? They wouldn't let me get near enough to make them hear, if I shouted my loudest. It's almost impossible for me to slip up on anyone, you know."

"Well, *I'll* tell them," she said decidedly.

"Oh, no! Please don't. You could never convince them. Promise me you won't. You know how mortals are."

"All right. Why," she added, realizing what he had said, "don't you think I'm a mortal?"

"I can tell by your eyes," said Branstookah.

It was true that Meira's eyes were not so blue as her mother's. They had a greenish light in them at times. It was the only indication of her fairy blood.

"Won't you have some lunch?" Branstookah said. "I'm sure you must be hungry after such a long ride."

"Thank you," she said. "Your house is lovely. I wouldn't have gone in, you know, if I hadn't thought it had been deserted for years."

"I understand," said the dragon. He led her into the house, and disappeared through a doorway concealed by hangings. In a few minutes he came back with a silver dish piled high with strange, luscious fruit, and tall silver goblets, frosted from the cold liquid they held.

The fruit was delicious, like nothing Meira had ever tasted. The goblets were filled with ice-cold nectar, and

the moment she drank of it all her weariness disappeared, and she felt as fresh as though she had not just taken a five-hour ride on horseback.

After lunch they wandered all over the mountaintop. Gorgeous butterflies floated past them, and birds sang in the trees. Branstookah showed her a lovely, lacy waterfall.

"When I want a bath I just get under it," he said. "Like this." He stepped into the waterfall, and the water made rainbows as it splashed on his many-colored scales.

The afternoon passed quickly, and Meira noticed with dismay that the shadows were long, and the sun was almost down.

"What shall I do?" she lamented. "Even if I had my pony I couldn't possibly get home before dark."

"I'll take you home," said Branstookah. "You can ride on my back, you know. I do hope you'll come again soon."

"I certainly will," Meira said.

"I'll send you a messenger," Branstookah said, "and you can write to me. I haven't had a letter for two hundred years, and I do love to get mail."

"Of course I will."

"A little pink bird," said the dragon. "He'll have a letter under his wing."

Having made these arrangements, they set out. Before she knew it Meira was sailing out over Kengaria, and in a very short time the dragon had landed gently on the palace roof.

CHAPTER 10

Kill the Dragon!

EVERYONE HAD BEEN VERY much worried about Meira when her pony came home without her, and when she surprised them by appearing inside the palace, they asked her many questions, but she wouldn't tell anyone where she had been, because she had promised Branstookah. King Ferdinand said she simply couldn't go riding any more without having someone with her.

So she went riding the next day with three grooms right behind her, taking care not to let her out of their sight. She hadn't gone very far when she saw Julian riding toward her.

"Hello!" he said. He turned his horse and rode along beside her, talking gaily as though he had seen her only yesterday.

Meira longed to tell him about Branstookah, but she

had promised, so she said nothing about it. Instead she answered his questions as to what she had been doing, and told him about Frederik and Johann.

"Are you going to marry one of those two?" he asked.

"I am not," Meira said decidedly.

"That's good," said Julian.

"Maybe you could come to the palace some time," Meira said.

"Thanks," said Julian. "I will, one of these days."

But he didn't come, and Meira didn't see him again for a week, though she rode every day.

"I wonder where he goes?" she thought. She thought about Julian a good deal. The more she thought about him, the more she wanted to see him.

One day she was on the palace roof, gazing longingly at the beautiful mountain, when she heard a soft twittering. She looked around, and there was a fat little pink bird.

"It must be Branstookah's messenger," she thought excitedly. She put out her hand, and the bird settled on her finger.

She felt under his wing, and sure enough there was a small slip of paper, tied with a blue ribbon. She untied it and opened the paper. It read:

WHAT ABOUT TEA ON WEDNESDAY AT FOUR?

"He writes very badly," she thought absently. "Wait just a minute," she told the little bird, and hurried down to her room for pen and ink. She turned the note over and wrote:

YOU'LL HAVE TO COME FOR ME. THEY WON'T LET ME OUT ALONE.

DON'T COME IF YOU THINK SOMEONE WILL SEE YOU.

She went back to the palace roof and tied the note under the little bird's wing again. He flew away, a little pink spot, soon lost in the distance.

On Wednesday Meira was on the palace roof a little before four, and soon she saw Branstookah flying toward her. She jumped upon his back as soon as he landed, and they were off.

"Aren't you afraid someone will see you?" she asked.

"I'm taking a chance," he said, "but they don't look up very often. I was so lonesome I couldn't help coming."

Meira had a wonderful afternoon on the mountain. Branstookah told her enthralling tales of dragons and enchantments, and lands far away, and everything he could think of.

Then, just as it was getting dark, they flew back to the palace, and no one knew she had been gone.

This went on for some time. Every few days Branstookah would come for her, and she would visit once more the Mount of the Dragons.

When she didn't visit Branstookah she rode about, and looked and looked for Julian, but he didn't come.

"What becomes of you?" Johann and Frederik asked her. "Do you go off and hide?"

"Ask me no questions," said Meira, and that was all she would tell them. She was happy now, because she had a wonderful secret to interest her, and, though she longed

to see Julian, she was sure he would come back sooner or later.

And then:

"There's a dragon been seen about here!" Johann told her one day excitedly, coming up to where she was sitting in the garden. "Think of it!"

Meira felt her hands grow cold. She clasped them tightly together and tried not to look concerned.

"There haven't been any dragons for years," she said.

"There's one now," said Johann. "A great many people have seen it."

"Well, what about it?" Meira asked.

"We must kill it, of course. Frederik and I and some soldiers are starting for the Mount early in the morning."

"How awful!" Meira cried. "Oh, you mustn't! I won't let you!"

"Why, Princess! Do you want to let a dragon run riot in the kingdom?"

"He won't run riot! He's been there for years! He's a vegetarian!"

Johann laughed heartily, and then looked at her, frowning. "What do you know about it?" he asked.

"I know all about it!" she cried. "You're always saying you love me. If you do, you'll leave the dragon alone."

"We can't possibly do that," Johann said.

Meira left him and ran across the garden, crying bitterly. "It's all my fault," she thought.

She wasn't looking where she was going, and ran right into Frederik, who said, "Did you hear about the dragon?"

"The dragon! They're going to kill him!"

"Don't be frightened, Meira," he said. "They'll have him killed in no time. Don't worry."

"I don't *want* him killed!" She ran into the palace, and found Queen Katrina and King Ferdinand having tea.

"Don't let them kill him!" she cried, throwing herself into her grandmother's arms in tears.

"Kill who?"

"The dragon! Branstookah!"

"What are you talking about, Meira?"

They listened silently while Meira told them about Branstookah, and that he was a vegetarian, and that everyone wanted to kill him. There wasn't any use keeping the secret any longer.

King Ferdinand shook his head, and said he'd see what he could do, but that if the Prime Minister and the Councilors wanted the dragon killed, he wasn't sure he could stop them.

"They're a bull-headed lot," he said. "But don't worry so. Branstookah probably isn't in as much danger as you think. I only hope he doesn't get annoyed and hurt anyone. I wish Mika were here."

Meira left them and roamed about the palace in a perfect frenzy, trying to think what to do.

She went back into the garden and tried to persuade Johann and Frederik not to go.

"I assure you, Princess," said Johann, "you're quite mistaken as to the nature of dragons. They're very fierce."

"You've never seen one," Meira said scornfully. "And

this particular dragon is a friend of mine. I know him."

Frederik coughed. "They—er—they say you've been seen riding on his back!" he managed to say at last. "Of course I know it's not true. . . ."

"It *is* true!" she said, exasperated. "Haven't I been telling you? I often go and have tea with him. That's how I know he's all right."

Johann and Frederik looked at each other.

"She is," said Frederik.

"I'm afraid so," Johann nodded.

"Is what?" asked Meira.

"Bewitched by the dragon," they said sadly, shaking their heads. "Everyone says so."

"Oh, go away!" Meira cried. "You're so stupid. Oh, I wish Julian were here! I certainly won't marry either one of you if you go near him. I am *not* bewitched!"

"You won't feel this way when we have killed him," they said. "Then the spell will be lifted from you."

Meira stamped her foot, and they went away, still determined to kill the dragon.

King Ferdinand came into the garden where they had been talking.

"The Council won't listen," he said. "I don't see how we can stop them from going. They think you're under a spell and that the only way to cure you is to kill the dragon."

"I hope Branstookah kills them all!" said Meira.

"If he did they'd send the whole army after him," said the King. "The only chance I see is for him to defeat them without hurting them and without getting killed himself. I'll see what I can think of tonight. They're not starting until morning, you know."

"Oh, Julian, where *are* you?" Meira thought miserably.

CHAPTER 11

Branstookah Besieged

EIRA TOSSED AND TURNED that night, worrying about Branstookah. She rose very early the next morning, and ran to find her grandfather.

Through the window, she saw Johann and Frederik at the head of a company of soldiers, starting for the Mount of the Dragons.

"Can't we possibly stop them?" she wailed.

"I could send soldiers to stop them," said the King, "but I can't have my people fighting each other. It might start a civil war. They feel very strongly about dragons. A strong enchantment about the mountain would do it, but I'm simply not enough of a magician. A dragon's a magic sort of creature. Doesn't Branstookah know any spells?"

"I'm afraid he isn't very well educated," Meira said. "He's just a plain sort of dragon."

She left the King and ran up to the roof, and looked and looked for the little pink bird. If it only happened that Branstookah sent her a message that day, she could write and warn him. But the bird was nowhere to be seen.

She had been watching for him for about an hour, when, looking down, she saw Julian riding into the courtyard. Julian! He had come! But suppose he wanted to kill the dragon too?

She rushed down the stairs and ran out and met him before he had time to dismount.

"Good morning," he said cheerfully. "I told you I'd come to see you."

"Oh, Julian, Julian, you must stop them!" Meira cried. "They've been gone over an hour! You must do something!"

"What are you talking about?" Julian asked.

"Don't you know about the dragon?"

"Haven't heard a word."

Meira rapidly told him her story. "Where have you *been?*" she said.

"There's no time to tell you now," he said. "I'll go and see what I can do."

He didn't think she was bewitched. He simply said he would help her, as soon as she asked him to.

"I knew you would," she said thankfully. "We must start this minute."

"We?" said Julian. "You're positively not going. Besides, I haven't time to wait for you. Good-by, darling."

Without giving her time to protest, he wheeled his horse and galloped away toward the Mount of the Dragons.

"I am too going," Meira said, and ran to get her pony.

Meira galloped along, her long braids of hair flying behind her. Then, realizing how far she had to go, she slowed to an easy canter. She didn't want to catch up with Julian, even if she could, as she was afraid he would try to send her home.

All the way to the mountain she was in a fever of anxiety, wondering what was happening to Branstookah and Julian, and hoping no one would hurt anyone else.

Through the blue flowers, she went, through the cloud and the purple flowers, and at last out into the sunshine among the pink fields. The road wasn't so steep here, and she urged her pony along.

As she approached Branstookah's house, Meira heard a noise of fighting and swords clashing against each other.

Someone yelled, "Look out, Branstookah! He nearly got you that time!" And Meira rode around a little hill onto the scene of the battle.

There was Branstookah, with Julian fighting beside him, and Johann and Frederik and some soldiers attacking them. As she watched, Branstookah rose in the air, swooped down upon his assailants, and picked up a soldier in his claws. He flew out of sight over the side of the mountain, leaving Julian, his back to the door of Branstookah's house, holding off with his sword as many of the soldiers as could get near enough to fight him.

In a few minutes Branstookah was back again, and as he flew down upon them, the soldiers scattered for a moment, only to come back and renew the attack. Johann and Frederik's company was handicapped by the fact that

There, standing in an ice-cold stream that ran through one corner of the room, she found a large urn filled with nectar.

Hastily she dipped a pitcher into it, and, snatching two goblets from a table, ran back into the other room.

Branstookah reached out a claw for a goblet, and managed to get it to his lips, but Julian was quite unconscious.

"Julian! Julian!" Meira sobbed, lifting his head, and trying to pour some of the drink into his mouth. She made him drink a few drops, then a little more, and in a few minutes he opened his eyes.

"Drink it," she urged him, and held the goblet to his lips. When he had drunk it, he could raise himself on one elbow.

She gave each of them another drink, and got water and cloths to tend their wounds.

Johann was muttering angrily to himself.

Meira stamped her foot. "Go home!" she said. "You've caused enough trouble for one day."

"You'll pay for this," Johann said to Branstookah. "You can't kill the subjects of Kengaria and not be punished."

Branstookah chuckled. "I didn't kill them," he said. "I set them down at the foot of my mountain. It will take them a long time to walk either back up here or home where they belong. It's pretty hard," he continued, "fighting someone you don't want to hurt, when he's trying to kill you."

"Johann, don't you know," said Julian, "that Branstookah could have knocked out half of your little company with one blow? Go home and tell them the truth, that the dragon isn't nearly so dangerous as a few men with the wrong idea in their heads."

Johann looked as though he thought it wasn't right for a dragon not to eat people, because that was the way dragons were supposed to be.

"You'd better let me take you home, Princess," he said.

Meira looked at him scornfully. "I wouldn't go anywhere with you," she said. "Bewitched, indeed!"

Johann looked at her a moment, then stalked out. Meira slammed the door hard behind him.

"There's some ointment on the lower shelf in the next room," Branstookah said. "I think it will help."

Meira went and got it. It was very much like the fairy ointment kept in the castle in the enchanted valley. She spread it on all their wounds, and soon Branstookah and Julian declared they felt much better, though somewhat weak.

There was a knock on the door, and Meira opened it, and there stood Mika.

"The battle seems to be over," he said. "King Ferdinand sent me a magic message, and I came as soon as I could."

"Welcome, Prince Mika," said Branstookah, knowing that that must be who he was.

Mika came in and they all sat down and drank nectar and ate some little cakes, and told him about the fight.

"I don't think there'll be any more trouble," Mika said. "This is a beautiful mountain you have here."

"Beautiful," said Julian. "Meira and I may build our

house here when we're married, if Branstookah doesn't mind."

"Married!" said Meira.

"We might discuss the wedding," said Julian.

"As Meira's aged father," said Mika, "I don't think I'm being consulted in the proper respectful manner."

"I'm not being consulted at all!" said Meira.

"If you refuse to look like an aged father," Julian said, "you can't expect people to remember to treat you as one."

"Have some cakes," said Branstookah.

"Branstookah says that hill over there," Julian went on, pointing through a small window, "can be made very roomy and comfortable."

"Hmmmmm," said Meira.

"I'm thinking of taking up magic and gardening," said Julian.

"Really?" said Meira.

"When your people come to visit us," he went on to Mika, "they ought to like this mountain, don't you think?"

"Very much," said Mika. "But I think I ought to know something about the bridegroom. Queen Katrina will think it odd if I can't tell her your name."

"It's Julian," said Meira.

"Prince Julian of Lucrania, the next kingdom west of here. My brother is king, and as he has six children there isn't much chance of my ever having to rule the country, so I ride around and see the world. It isn't much fun just sitting around being brother to a king, you know."

"Then you were in Lucrania?" Meira asked.

"Yes. I had to go home on business, and that's why I couldn't come to see you sooner," said Julian. "We'll have an outdoor wedding," he went on. "A wedding under the trees, on a carpet of pink blossoms." He looked sidewise at Meira.

She was silent a moment. "Maybe I will marry you after all," she said.

"Would you like to see my vegetable garden?" Branstookah said to Mika. "Gardening is a hobby of mine." They slipped out.

Lucy rubbed her eyes. She felt as though she had been dreaming. The little dog stretched and yawned.

Michael put his arm about her shoulders. Together they watched the moving shadows, which grew plain and strong again as soon as he stopped speaking.

"I'd *love* to see that mountain," she whispered.

"You'll dream about it," Michael said. "That's almost as good."

"Meira's shadow is not here?" she asked.

"No. You see, she lived as a mortal. She loved the mortals best. The people to whom the shadows belong are all in Fairyland. Meira stayed in Kengaria, and lived in a beautiful house like the dragon's, only smaller, on the Mount of the Dragons. Later they built the royal palace there."

"Why?"

"You see, old King Ferdinand had no heir, no one to rule the country after him. His only child, Gloria, had married into the fairy line, so her husband, Mika, couldn't rule over a mortal kingdom. Then his grandson, Robin, loved the fairies best, and he couldn't succeed to the throne either.

"Of course King Ferdinand was delighted when Meira married a mortal, and he made Julian and Meira his heirs. Years later, when the old king died, they became King and Queen, and their sons and daughters ruled after them. It was a long, long time ago.

"Meira and Julian couldn't bear to leave the mountain, so they had the royal palace built there, and told their subjects they would just have to stop being afraid to go to the Mount of the Dragons.

"Branstookah was very happy and not lonely any more, and Julian could keep an eye on his kingdom by riding all over it on Branstookah's back, and see that everything was all right."

As he stopped speaking, Lucy noticed that the light was dim, not only because it was becoming dense and misty purple, but because there wasn't as much light from the window as there had been. It was getting late.

"Oh, dear," she said, "I've just got to get home before dark. Grandma will be worried if I don't."

"You shall," said Michael.

"But what about the dark tunnel?"

"I'll see that the goblins there don't hurt you."

"Then do you think—could you tell me one more story before I go?"

Michael got up and looked out of the window again. "A short one," he said. "I think there's time. I'd like to keep

you until the last few minutes. It keeps me from being so impatient."

"Impatient?" Lucy asked.

"Be silent," Michael said.

Lucy was silent. She was beginning to like the queer, whispering stillness and the slight feeling of giddiness that came to her from the swirling purple air. The stillness and the shadows and the strange, dreamy feeling; the cobwebs stirred by not a breath of air, and the streams of dim light from the window.

CHAPTER 12

The Shadow Room

FTER MEIRA WAS MAR-
ried (Michael said) Gloria and Mika came back to the
enchanted valley and lived in the castle with Robin and
Bluebell for many years, and were very happy.

Then the King of Blue Elfland decided to retire. As
the Princess Bluebell was his only child, she and Robin
went to Blue Elfland to rule over the kingdom. Of course
they took their six children with them, and Mika and
Gloria were left alone in the castle.

One day they were walking in the garden.

"I'm eighty years old today," Gloria said. "I ought to
be an old woman. Are the mirrors enchanted, or is it
really true?"

"It's really true, darling," Mika said, kissing her.

"Mika!" Gloria said. "I—I feel so queer. There's something the matter with me. Mika. . . ."

Mika looked at her in alarm. She did look queer—pale. She was looking at him with an anxious expression on her face, growing paler and paler, not just her face, but all of her.

A great sadness descended on him, and tears came into his eyes. He took a hurried step toward her, to hold her in his arms. He reached out—and there was nothing there! There was just a stirring of the air, and a faint, frightened cry of "Mika!" Gloria was gone.

Mika was so distracted he hardly knew what he was doing. He walked up and down, up and down. Gloria was gone! He called her name, but she didn't answer.

He had known it would happen. He knew that now she was waiting for him in Fairyland, according to the spell that had been made so long ago.

The long years stretched before him, centuries until he could see her again. For centuries he would have to remain in his mortal form, waiting, waiting, and never seeing her.

For a week he hardly ate or slept, and then Flumpdoria appeared at the castle, as he paced about in the garden.

"Mika," she said. "Behave yourself. You knew this would happen. You'll have to be patient, dear. When Gloria knows you're unhappy, it makes her more unhappy than she is already."

"Can't she ever come and see me?" Mika asked.

"You know she can't. She must abide by the enchantment. But I can come, or anyone except Gloria. We'll bring you news of her."

"I'll try to get used to it," Mika said.

"Gloria sends her dearest love," said Flumpdoria, "and says to remember she's always there, waiting. I must get back. There are so many things I must show Gloria."

"Good-by, Flumpy. Thanks for coming. Come to see me whenever you can."

"I certainly will," said Flumpdoria.

Some days later, having nothing to do, Mika thought he would explore the castle and go in rooms he hadn't visited for years.

He started at the top, but he never got past one room, for the very highest room in the castle is the tower room, and that's the first one he went in.

He went in and sat down, thinking of how happy he and Gloria had been.

Then he noticed that the air was turning purple. Not much light came from the window, and everything was dim. There was a faint whispering and sighing, and shadows moved about. He didn't move or make a sound, but just sat there, watching.

He felt that there was something familiar about the shadows. He looked and looked and saw—Gloria!

She was walking about and seemed to be weeping. He never took his eyes from her. After a while she dried her eyes and sat down. She seemed to be thinking and didn't move.

One by one Mika recognized the other shadows. Robin, Bluebell, and their six children—every one of his family who had lived in the castle and were there no more.

They passed and repassed each other, so that at times it was hard to recognize them.

"I believe those are shadows of what they're doing now," Mika thought. "They've left their shadows behind. Now I can see what Gloria is doing on any sunny day in Fairyland. It's almost as good as being with her."

There was someone missing, Meira.

"Of course," he thought. "She's a mortal now. She has her shadow with her. Naturally it wouldn't be here."

Mika spent the whole day in the shadow room, and a good deal of his time after that.

"I don't understand it," Flumpdoria said when he told her about it the next time she came to see him. "No one knew that would be part of the spell. It must be a great comfort to you."

It was a great comfort to him at first, but after a while he couldn't bear to go up there. Seeing Gloria's shadow only made him long for her more.

Flumpdoria and King Klux and Queen Meira, and Robin and Bluebell, and all Mika's friends spent as much time with him as they could, trying to keep him from being lonely, but Mika wasn't very cheerful company.

After a while he decided to travel, and through all the long years he roamed the world. He always attended the christenings of the babies of the royal family of Kengaria, and watched them grow up, and king after king ascend the throne.

These kings and queens were his great- and great-great- and great-great-great-grandchildren, but he didn't have much fun with them. Sometimes he didn't even ap-

pear but stood about in his cloak of invisibility, just to
see that everything was all right.

They were so *very* mortal. As the centuries passed, the
art of magic was gone from the kingdom. It made him
sad that the people of Kengaria didn't even believe in it
any more.

Branstookah was always glad to see him. He was lonely
again. For two or three hundred years the royal palace
had stood on his mountain, but finally it had been moved
back, and a new castle built where King Ferdinand's had
been.

"No one ever comes here any more," Branstookah told
him. "I really believe they doubt my existence. Anyway,
they don't bother me," he added. "Sometimes I wish they
would. I get bored."

The time was so long, not like time in Fairyland, where
a year passed so quickly one hardly noticed it was gone.
As the slow centuries rolled on, Mika was lonely, lonely.

There were too many mortals. They built their towns
right outside the enchanted valley. Of course they didn't
know about the valley. They never came in.

Michael stopped talking, and Lucy looked up. "Is that
all?" she asked.

Michael stood up. "It's all there's time for, little Lucy.
You must go, right away. Look."

Lucy looked, and saw that the shadows were all running about, waving their arms excitedly.

"What're they doing, Michael?"

"They know it's almost time," Michael said. "We must hurry."

Lucy took a last look at the wonderful shadow room as they went through the door, and then they were going down again, down the steep, narrow stairs hung with cobwebs.

Michael hurried her through the castle and out into the valley.

"There's not much time," he said. "I'm very glad you came, Lucy. I've enjoyed your visit."

"Time for what?" Lucy said.

Michael paid no attention. "You must take Flumpy with you," he said hurriedly. "I give him to you. Go with Lucy, Flumpy."

He was slipping a ring off his finger. He took her hand and slipped the ring on her middle finger. The ring, which had fitted Michael, became smaller as it slipped onto Lucy's hand and fitted her small finger as though it had been made for it.

She stared at it wonderingly.

"Always wear this ring," Michael said. "Never take it off. You may come back to the enchanted valley whenever you want to. But it will be different. It will always be different."

"Oh, may I?" Lucy exclaimed delightedly.

"Some time you may want to bring someone with you," Michael went on, "but if he or she isn't the kind of person who should enter the enchanted valley, you will never find the tunnel while he is with you. You can tell by the ring. If you touch someone with the ring, and it glows with a fairy fire, you'll know he is the kind of person you may take into the valley."

Suddenly Michael turned and started back into the castle.

"Run, Lucy," he said urgently. "Run! Go through the tunnel. The ring will protect you from the goblins. Hurry! The time is up!"

Lucy didn't know what he meant, but she ran as fast as she could toward the tunnel, and stopped only when she had reached the goblin grass that grew in front of it. There she turned for a last look at the enchanted valley.

It was getting dark, and the strange green-blue sky seemed to toss about, flowing back and forth as though it were water instead of air. The goblin grass waved, although there was no wind. There was no sound anywhere.

She looked at the castle and at Michael standing in front of it, waving to her.

As she stood gazing at it, the castle simply disappeared. It wasn't there any more. It was gone. Michael was gone, too. Lucy was looking out over a valley of grass and trees and far mountains and—nothing, nothing else.

Then she knew. She waved her hand toward where the castle had been.

"Good-by, Michael!" she called softly. "Good-by, Mika! I'm glad the thousand years are up. I'll come back and see you."

Then she turned and ran as fast as she could through the dark tunnel, with Flumpy at her heels.

"That's why he was in a hurry," Lucy thought as she ran along. "Suppose I had been in the castle when it went away? I wonder. . . ."

The sun was almost down when Lucy reached home, although she had run most of the way.

"Where have you been, child?" her grandmother asked. "I was beginning to worry about you. Why, what's this?"

"This is Flumpdoria," Lucy said. "He's mine. Mika gave him to me. I expect he's a human dog, and couldn't go to Fairyland."

"Whatever are you talking about?" Grandma exclaimed, as she shook hands with Flumpy, who had put up a paw.

So Lucy told her the whole story. "And I'm sure he's Mika himself," she finished, "and the thousand years and seven days must have been over, because the castle went away, and he did too, and now he's with Gloria again, and I'm so glad!"

Grandma sat a long time gazing in silence at the magic ring, after Lucy had told her everything.

"It's a lucky thing to be a friend of the little people," she said at last. "But when you go back to the enchanted valley you must tell me, dear. I must always know where you are."

She sighed and said that Lucy must go to bed now.

That night in her bed, Lucy felt the magic ring on her finger and wondered what she would find when she went again to the enchanted valley. Michael—Mika—had said it would all be different.